Ride for Hell Pass

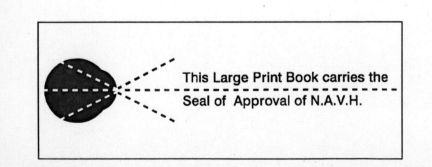

This Large Print Book carries the
Seal of Approval of N.A.V.H.

RIDE FOR HELL PASS

ARTHUR HENRY GOODEN

WHEELER PUBLISHING
A part of Gale, Cengage Learning

GALE
CENGAGE Learning·

• New Haven, Conn • Waterville, Maine • London

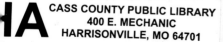

GALE
CENGAGE Learning

LIBRARY OF CONGRESS CATALOGING-IN-PUBLICATION DATA

Gooden, Arthur Henry, 1879–1971.
  Ride for hell pass / by Arthur Henry Gooden.
    page ; cm. — (Wheeler Publishing large print western)
  ISBN-13: 978-1-4104-5816-2 (softcover)
  ISBN-10: 1-4104-5816-4 (softcover)
  1. Large type books. I. Title.
PS3513.O4767R53 2013
813'.52—dc23   2013003469

Published in 2013 by arrangement with Golden West Literary Agency.

Printed in the United States of America
  1 2 3 4 5   17 16 15 14 13

TO THOSE DAYS

CHAPTER ONE

The horse was more than willing to halt after the steep climb from the canyon floor. Hill Carnady got down stiffly from his saddle, gave the weary buckskin a sympathetic slap. They had put a lot of miles behind them since early dawn, most of them over rugged country that had tested endurance close to the exhaustion point. The stage road out of Hatchita would have been easier travelling, but Hill had reasons to believe that the more remote, seldom-used trails offered considerably less danger.

His gaze went to the distant mountain peaks now starkly limned against the sunset's flaring back-drop. Clouds were pushing up from the south, spreading a dark blanket over the evening sky.

Hill's weather-wise eyes appraisingly studied the thunderheads. He had been away for more than a year, but this southwestern corner of the Territory of New

Mexico was his own country and he was deeply interested in the portents. The fast-approaching storm promised an end to the long drought. He had never seen the landscape so parched. The usual summer thunder showers through July into September would be manna from heaven for rancher and cattleman alike.

A last, brief gleam of sunlight broke through the cloud mass, and Hill's eyes narrowed in a sharp look at the lifting dust brought to his attention by that momentary bit of sunshine. Horsemen were approaching up the trail from the valley. And horsemen *could* mean danger — disaster.

He was almost instantly in motion, leading the horse across the boulder-strewn bluff to a heavy growth of stunted juniper trees. Darkness was coming fast, hastened by the clouds now blanketing the last of the sunset.

Aware of a warm feeling of gratitude for that betraying glint of sunlight on the lifting dust, Hill pushed through the clawing junipers into a small clearing walled on three sides by huge granite boulders. He tied the horse, examined the gun in his holster and made his way cautiously through the brush to another boulder that lay some ten yards from the trail. He wanted a look at those approaching riders, if it could be managed in that growing darkness. It could be that they were merely innocent passers-by. Possibly, but hardly probable. Men riding on honest business were not likely to use this long abandoned and dangerous trail.

Lightning flared over the mountains, thunder growled. Hill continued to crouch close to the juniper-screened boulder, gaze intent on the trail at a point where the unknown horsemen would finish their climb and appear on the bluff.

His thoughts went to the disturbing letter that had reached him in Denver. He had burned the letter but remembered every word Sam Hally had written.

It's time you hit the trail for Hell Pass. Something is awful wrong at the ranch and it looks like your grandpa is needing you. Seth and me was out there but was told the old Captain couldn't see us because he was too sick. Seth and me wasn't liking it at all. We've rode stirrup to stirrup with Cap Carnady too many years for him not to see us no matter how sick he is. You ride for Hell Pass on the jump. One of us will be on the watch for you at Coldwater.

Hill's ears suddenly picked up the sound of shod hoofs labouring up the steep ascent. It was a hard climb and the horses were taking it easy. His thoughts went back to the letter, to the laconic postscript Seth McGee had scrawled.

Watch your step, son. There's wolves on your trail.

Something like an affectionate grin momentarily softened Hill Carnady's grim-set mouth. He could visualize those two old-timers; big Sam Hally, with his gentle voice and smile, slow to anger, but terrible in his wrath. And his rotund little partner, Seth McGee, whose cherubic look was entirely deceptive. That pair of formidable, hard-bitten old cowmen would not have written such an urgent letter without good reason.

Lightning flared again, thunder crashed and reverberated from crag to crag. And in the ensuing stillness he could hear the slow-moving horses. A few more minutes would bring the riders up on the bluff.

Hill drew the .45 from its holster, eyes alert now for the oncoming strangers, his troubled thoughts still with Sam's letter — and his grandfather. He had hated to leave Denver. His one year of study at the School of Mines had been valuable but he needed more knowledge if he hoped to successfully prospect the mineral possibilities of the ranch. His grandfather had scoffed at such possibilities, told him not to spoil a good cowman by chasing fool rainbows. A year now, since he had braved his grandfather's displeasure. A lot could happen in a year, and judging from Sam's letter, a lot *had* happened. One thing was certain, it was imperative for him to get back to the ranch as quickly and inconspicuously as possible. It seemed that unknown enemies were on the watch for him. He wished that Seth McGee's warning postscript had been less laconic.

The horsemen were visible now, vague shapes in the darkening night, two of them, moving slowly along the narrow, stony trail. The rider in the lead reined to a standstill and Hill heard his voice, gruff, complaining.

"Was beginning to think we'd never get up here," he said. "The boss was crazy in the head, thinking the fellow would head this way out of Painted Canyon."

"She ees bad trail," agreed his companion. He swore feelingly in Spanish.

"I figger we're the first fools to make that climb in ten years," grumbled the first speaker. He eased from his saddle, stood spraddle-legged, fingers fumbling tobacco and papers from a shirt pocket. "Washed out so bad even a goat would look cross-eyed at it. My bronc started to slide over more'n once."

The second rider swore again, got down from his saddle. "More worse w'en we go down canyon." He drew a flask from his pocket. "A dreenk mooch good now, you bet."

"Ain't headin' down into the canyon," declared the other man. "Not in this dark." He reached out a hand for the flask. "Can use a slug my own self, Pedro."

The Mexican surrendered the flask, began making a cigarette. "Beeg rain come queek, no." His voice showed worry. "W'at we do, Topaz?"

"We're staying up here on the rimrock," Topaz said. "We're a heap safer up here than down in the canyon if a cloudburst hits." He took another drink from the flask, handed it back. "Should be some place where we can rig our tarps for shelter. Cain't see much in this dark."

Lightning flared over the scene, drew a startled grunt from the Mexican; and as the thunder went bellowing into the distance, Hill heard an exclamation from Topaz. "Did you see it, Pedro, when the sky lit up? A bunch of junipers, yonder, and slabs of rock as big as a house. You go scout over there, Pedro."

The Mexican showed reluctance. "Thees hombre we look for," he reminded. "He may be here — make ambush for us."

"That Carnady jasper ain't no fool like me and you," Topaz said bitterly. "He was raised in these parts. He'd be too smart to risk breaking his neck on *this* trail. Get a move on, Pedro. We got to rig our tarps awful fast."

Hill was aware of cold prickles chasing up and down his spine. Pedro would find the buckskin horse cached in those junipers; also the Mexican's vague shape was approaching at an angle that would bring him within a scant yard of where he crouched close to the boulder thinly screened by the brush.

Hill held down his rising panic, took his one chance, fired, not at the unsuspecting Mexican but at the shadowy form of Topaz standing near the horses. Lightning again flared as he squeezed the trigger, threw a brief white glare over the scene. Pedro whirled, glimpsed Topaz lifting his gun to answer the mysterious shot that had spurted dust up in his face. "You try for keel me!"

he yelled. His gun spat flame as Topaz fired twice.

A deep hush followed the gunshots. Hill slowly got to his feet, aware of a growing amazement as he stared, incredulous, at the Mexican's still form lying only a few yards away. He had taken his one desperate chance to create a diversion, and thanks to the lightning had escaped the death that had reached too uncomfortably close. Pedro had not noticed the spurt of flame from Hill's .45, perhaps because his attention was drawn by the first fork of lightning splintering the blackness above. He had heard the shot, and under the lightning's glare, glimpsed Topaz, gun in lifted hand. To misunderstand was natural. Topaz was deliberately trying to kill him. His immediate reaction was fatal to both.

A drop of rain splashed on Hill's face. He came out of his trance, moved slowly to the shape sprawled against a thorny bush. A look told him that the Mexican was dead. More drops of rain splashed hard on his face. The deluge was about due. Common sense indicated a hasty return to his horse for his slicker, caution urged him across the few yards to where the other vaguely-seen shape lay in that darkness. There was just a chance that Topaz was not dead. If there was life still in him it was imperative to know it. He could not risk the desperado escaping to carry the tale back to the man who had sent him and the Mexican to do murder. There was no doubt about the intentions of these hired killers. Topaz had spoken his name. . . . *that Carnady jasper . . .* Topaz knew who he was and would have shot him to death on sight — from ambush.

The two horses snorted as he approached, lifted their heads in a suspicious look at him. He spoke, softly, reassuringly; and sensing he meant no harm they stood quiet, heads drooping wearily.

Hill bent over the still form lying near them. His quick look told him the man was dead. The Mexican's panic-flung bullet had taken Topaz between the eyes. Lightning ripped through the darkness, fleetingly revealed the slain desperado's face, a face Hill failed to recognize. He turned away to the horses, aware of a sick feeling in him. Two dead men who wore the names of Topaz and Pedro — strangers who had been sent to ambush him. The sick feeling hardened into fierce anger.

He stood for a moment, heedless of the increasing downpour. The horses were frightened, trembling under the shocking impact of the thunder. He was sorry for them, also undecided about what to do with them. He only knew that he could not yet allow them to return to wherever they came from — betray the fate of their riders.

Without another glance at the dead man, Hill snatched up dangling reins, went stumbling through the darkness, the two horses following at his heels.

Intermittent lightning helped show the way back to the big clump of junipers. The buckskin nickered softly as he led the horses inside the granite-walled enclosure. He jerked his slicker from saddle, shrugged into it. The rain was really coming down, now, an ear-shattering, deafening roar against the background of crackling thunder. Hill hastily unrolled his tarpaulin and flung it over the buckskin, mainly to keep his saddle and rifle dry. He blessed the little refuge he had found. The great boulders kept the rain from beating in, and the thick-branched junipers did a lot to break the nearly vertical deluge. In a few minutes, though, he was standing ankle deep in water.

He was in a fever of impatience to be on his way down to the valley. The fact that two men had been sent to waylay him increased his alarm about his grandfather. Also it was imperative that he reached Coldwater before the failure of Topaz and Pedro to return with news of him aroused speculations as to their fate. The trail was going to be dangerous, badly washed by the cloudburst, and the darkness would not make the going any easier.

There was nothing he could do, except hold his impatience in check, wait for the storm to subside. He was familiar with these summer thunder showers and was reasonably sure that an hour or two would find a clearing sky; and with the rolling back of the clouds there would be moonlight. Already the thunder was fading into the distance and the furious drive of the rain was perceptibly less.

Visibility was growing in the little enclosure under the junipers. The moon had found a break in the clouds. Hill looked thoughtfully at the slain men's rain-soaked horses. It was a temptation to leave them tied in the brush near where their dead riders lay on the trail. The picture would be convincing — a quarrel — Topaz and Pedro shooting it out. The position of their bodies; the single empty shell in the Mexican's gun, two empty shells in the other man's gun; the single bullet that had taken Topaz between the eyes, the two bullets that had smashed the life from Pedro. Anybody sent to look for the missing desperadoes would carry back only one story. Topaz and Pedro had for some unknown reason gone *loco* and shot each other to death, leaving their horses tied in the brush.

Hill's troubled frown deepened. He was not wasting pity on Topaz and Pedro. The fate of their horses was a different problem. If he left them tied in the brush it might be days before searchers followed the trail up to the bluffs. The unfortunate animals could starve to death — die of thirst.

Moonlight flowed through the dripping junipers, and standing there, wondering what to do, Hill was almost startled by the sudden hush after the storm. The only sound that came from the night was the soft music of countless rills tumbling down the slopes, the distant, muted roar of flooding arroyos. Nothing to keep him from heading down-trail now. Only the problem of the horses.

He stripped his tarp from the buckskin, shook off the water, rolled it and tied it to his saddle. If he turned the horses loose they would soon find their way back to the home ranch, or livery barn, which would mean an immediate search for their missing riders. His only alternative was to take them with him to Coldwater — turn them over to Sam Hally or Seth McGee. He had another good reason for holding on to the horses. The brands they wore might be a clue that could lead him to the man who owned them — the employer of two dead would-be killers.

His decision made, Hill led the three horses from the enclosure, got into his saddle and rode across the rimrock to the down-trail. The buckskin, snorting, cautious, splashed through pools of water, the confiscated horses following on a lead-rope. The moon, a day past full, was well above the clouds still massed over the mountains, threw a soft, silver glow over the scene, touched the still shapes of the dead men lying on the stony hillocks where they had fallen. Hill gave them a troubled look as he rode past. There was nothing he could do for them. Time was precious and his one objective now must be to reach Coldwater where Sam Hally or Seth McGee would be waiting for him.

CHAPTER TWO

He pushed on down the trail, the two horses following reluctantly on the lead-rope. The slope was alive with countless rushing little streams. Shod hoofs dug into mud, struck sparks from uncovered granite. Twice he was forced to dismount, detour around slides of dirt and boulders. He blessed the revealing moonlight, the sure-footed horse under him.

A last ridge dropped him down from the foothill country and he swung south, following the outside bend of a creek that a few hours earlier was a wide sandy wash but now was spilling a roaring, muddy flood over its low banks. The moon looked down from a star-filled sky, filled the willow brakes with phantom lights and shadows. Hill had often hunted here. Doves and quail — ducks, and once he had shot a mountain lion that had wandered down from the hills. He was only fifteen, and his surprise encounter with the big cat had given him a fright he still remembered. The sight of the mangled remains of a calf had enraged him, stiffened his courage, and the first bullet from his new Winchester had been enough. He had kept the hide for years, stretched on his bedroom wall, until Teresa rebelled and made him throw it away because of its mangy condition. The thought of the kindly old Mexican woman was another spur to his anxiety. Teresa had nursed him and mothered him from infancy to manhood. He was still her *muchacho*. Trouble for his grandfather would mean trouble for Teresa, too. Or else she was dead, beyond reach of the mysterious danger that threatened the old Carnady ranch.

The creek made a leisurely swing to the west, and growing excitement made Hill forget his weariness. He knew that the creek emptied into the west fork of the San Jacinto River, just around the next bend. And beyond the West Fork lay the vast Carnady range that reached almost to the Mexican border.

He frowningly recalled Sam Hally's letter. Sam had made it plain enough that he or Seth would be waiting for him at Coldwater. He felt inclined to disobey. Another hour's ride would bring him to the home ranch — to his grandfather. He thought of Seth McGee's ominous postscript. *Watch your step, son. There's wolves on your trail. . . .* The affair up on the rimrock was grim proof that Seth knew what he was talking about.

Hill shook his head, reluctantly abandoned the impulse to disregard Sam's instructions. Sam and Seth were a pair of wary old longhorns. There must be some good reason why they wanted him at Coldwater.

He could see the river now, a silver flood under the moon. He saw something else that made him bring the buckskin to a standstill, a faint, yellow gleam about a mile beyond the fork, on his side of the stream.

Surprise widened his eyes. This was his own country, as familiar as the palm of his hand. That yellow gleam was lamplight and came from a house that had not been at Red Butte Springs hardly more than a year ago. He had often made camp there. The Springs were a never-failing source of good water, even in the dry seasons when the San Jacinto was little more than a sandy wash.

The buckskin horse showed signs of impatience, an eagerness to be moving. He sensed a barn not far distant. Hill quieted him. "Easy, Buck," he said. "We've got to think this thing out." He reached for tobacco sack and papers in his shirt pocket, realized he was still wearing his slicker. He got down from the saddle, pulled the slicker off, rolled it and tied it to the saddle. The two horses on the lead rope were showing impatience, too, he noticed as he shaped and lit his cigarette. His gaze returned to the lighted window some two miles up the slope from the river, but little more than a mile from where he stood. It could mean anything — hospitality — or danger; and it came to him at that moment that he could use a little hospitality. The difficulties of the trail had tired him, and he was ravenous for food. The horse, too, was in poor shape for the remaining ten miles to Coldwater.

He deliberated for the length of his cigarette. He could stick close to the willow brakes, continue on to Comanche Pass, make Coldwater by dawn, or head up the slope towards that beckoning light in the window. He knew by the moon, without looking at his watch, that it was close to nine o'clock. One other thing he knew. He would have to make sure that it was hospitality he would find up there on the slope — *not danger.*

Weariness, hunger — curiosity, decided him. He flipped his cigarette into a muddy pool, turned to step into his saddle, hesitated, looked back at the horses on the lead-rope. It was his first real look at them and he had a disturbing feeling that he had seen them before, the bay with the white blaze on its nose, the red roan. It was possible that the moon was bright enough for him to read the brands they wore. No need to wait for daylight.

He went to them, stared closely at the marks left by the branding iron. His heart began to pound. The marks were unmistakable, the HC — the Carnady ranch brand. No wonder that the horses were familiar to him.

He stood for long moments, a sickness in his eyes. Sam Hally was right. Something was indeed very wrong at the ranch. He understood now why Sam wanted him at Coldwater. The fact that the roads, the trails, were being watched meant that his appearance at the ranch would be his death warrant.

Hill got into his saddle, swung left from the trail, up the long slope towards Red Butte Springs where the lighted window beckoned against the dark background of cottonwood trees. He found the short-cut trail he had often used when camping up there, little more than a cow-path, kept the buckskin moving at a slow walk, his eyes wary, ears alert. For all he knew he could be riding into a trap from which there would be no escape.

He came to barbed wires strung to newly-cut poles, swung right towards a thick clump of huge cottonwoods, slid from his saddle and tied the horses inside the screening branches.

No sound broke the stillness of the moon-lit night, only the muted roar of the distant river, running bank full. Hill stepped into the moonlight, slid under the barbed wires and reached the concealment of more cottonwoods within some twenty yards of the lighted window. He stood there, studying what he saw under the light of the full moon. A small, frame house, a stove-pipe elbowing from a little lean-to in the rear; a new house, lacking paint or whitewash. The barn, inside the pole corral, was new, too, and larger than the house. His look went to the plough that rested against a small pile of lumber, took in the light ranch-wagon — the buckboard covered with a canvas sheet. Everything new, and all of it crying out the word *homesteader.*

Hill frowned, recalled something his grandfather had said more than once. . . . *Should get title to that Red Butte Springs section before some homesteader files on it. . . .*

It seemed that some homesteader had got the jump on old Captain Carnady. If those neat buildings and equipment meant anything at all they meant that the springs were no longer on HC range.

It came to Hill as he stood there that there was a lot of HC range open to homesteaders, a fact that his grandfather had often wryly admitted. *The nation is getting land hungry, boy. No use trying to stem the tide. Means a lot of big bites taken from old HC. No sense for us to kick against the pricks . . . There'll be plenty of range left for you to carry on.*

Hill's thoughtful gaze went back to the house, to the lamplit windows. A homesteader would not be back of the mysterious danger that threatened the Carnady ranch — its big-hearted owner. His grandfather was not the man to ride rough-shod over a man using his lawful rights. It did not seem possible that homesteading Red Butte Springs could be the cause of the trouble that had Sam and Seth so worried. And yet, for all he knew — that little house could mean danger — *death* — if he sought hospitality there.

A sound suddenly broke the stillness of the night. Hill could hardly believe his ears. Organ music — a harmonium — a girl's voice, lilting — joyous. He knew the words. An old Thanksgiving Day hymn.

We plough the fields, and scatter
    The good seed on the land,
But it is fed and watered
    By God's almighty hand.

Hill listened, spell-bound, wondering. A Thanksgiving Day hymn in July. But why? The answer was not hard. The storm — the needed rain.

The clear young voice was finishing the verse with an enthusiasm that put a lump in his throat.

All good gifts around us
    Are sent from heaven above;
Then thank the Lord, O thank the Lord
For all his love.

A few soft organ notes, then again the silence of the night, touched only by the muted roar of the river. Hill was already moving towards the kitchen door. He was sure of one thing now. No danger lurked in that little house.

He rapped lightly, heard a quick stir, and then the girl's voice, low, startled.

"Who is it?"

Ordinarily Hill would not have hesitated. He knew that his grandfather was prepared to accept these intrusions on HC range. Sam Hally had called him home because of some mysterious danger that threatened the ranch — the old cattleman. It seemed a poor time to divulge his identity.

The girl's voice came again, sharp, hostile. "I have a gun ——"

He said apologetically, "I'm sorry if I startled you, I've been riding all day and got caught in that thunderstorm. Saw your light and it seemed a good idea to head in for your yard."

"Oh, dear!" There was worry in her voice — uncertainty. 'Where are you from, and where are you going?" A brief pause. "And who are you, anyway?"

"My name is Hill," he said, truthfully enough. "From Santa Fé, with business in Coldwater."

Another long silence. She was evidently thinking it over. Hill said, his tone purposely rueful, "Well — I'll be moving on. Sorry to have troubled you."

"Wait a moment ——" And then, a hint of pity mingled with the worry in her voice, "I suppose you're starving."

"I haven't eaten since sun-up," admitted Hill. "I'd have been in Coldwater tonight if

28

the storm hadn't held me up."

"It was wonderful," the girl said from her side of the door. "We were needing rain, *oh, so much!*"

"I heard you singing that Thanksgiving hymn," Hill told her. "It was one reason why I turned in here."

"Do you know that old Thanksgiving hymn?" Her voice sounded pleased — relieved.

"Known it just about all my life," Hill said. His answer, his low laugh seemed to be deciding in his favour. He wished she would open the door. He wanted a look at this girl whose voice so unaccountably captured his imagination.

"Put your horse in the barn." She paused. "I'll have some stew heated up in a jiffy, and coffee ready."

"You are very kind." Hill turned from the door. He decided it was best not to mention the two horses on the lead rope. He glanced back as he moved across the yard, saw the lamplight suddenly dim out, understood the reason. The girl wanted a glimpse of him in the moonlight. He hoped he didn't look too tough; gaunt, mud-spattered, a two day's bristle on his face.

He decided to risk taking all three horses into the barn. She might or might not be

29

watching. He would have to think up some story if she questioned him about the two extra horses.

The lights were on again in the house when he led the horses across the corral and into the barn. There were no stalls, just a long manger running from end to end. He stripped off bridles, forked a sparse helping of hay into the manger. The barn and everything in it shrieked of newness, even the boards had the smell of freshly-cut lumber. He counted five horses lined up at the manger, a pair of work animals for the plough he had noticed in the yard, a pair of matched bays for the buckboard, and a good-looking saddle mare, a chestnut with a star on her forehead. It all depressed him. So much hope, here, a hope born of innocence — ignorance.

Hill scowled, shook his head, impatient with himself. He was wrong. This little homestead was the blossoming of bright courage, the same gallant challenge to the wilderness that had animated his own pioneering grandfather. The first little herd of longhorns driven up from the Brazos, Indians, rustlers, border renegades — droughts. A lot of boldness and fortitude and indomitable resolution had gone into the winning of the great Carnady cattle ranch from a hostile land.

She must have been listening for his step. The door opened, and she stood there, a dark-haired girl whose face tilted up at him in a grave, appraising look. Apparently the appraisal satisfied her. She gave him a faint smile.

"Please come in, Mr. Hill." She stood aside, her eyes taking in his tall, hard lean body, the reddish brown hair, the eyes startlingly dark blue in the deeply tanned face. Her gaze lowered to the mud-spattered high-heeled boots. "You're a cowman?"

Hill dropped his Stetson on a chair, smiled back at her. "All my life ——" His look made a quick survey of the neat little kitchen, came back to her, his smile apologetic. "I picked up a lot of mud on the trail. Hate to be dragging it in here."

"I'd rather have a little mud than all the dust we've been having." She gestured at the table. "Sit down, Mr. Hill. The coffee is about ready." She moved across the room to the stove, removed a lid and poked a piece of mesquite down in the red embers. She lifted the cover from an iron pot, stirred the contents with a big spoon. "I suppose even a cowman will eat lamb stew — if he's hungry?" Her head turned in a brief look at him.

"I'm not one of those cowmen who object to sheep," Hill assured her.

"Most of you cowmen *do* object." She faced him from the stove, and the lamplight gave him his first real look at her eyes, grey, with hazel lights and at this moment, hot with indignation. "We've been warned there'll be trouble if — if we run sheep here." She turned back to the iron kettle, began spooning its contents into a bowl.

She placed the bowl of stew in front of him, sliced some bread and poured coffee into a heavy mug. "No cream," she said. "Our one cow strayed, or has been stolen." The hint of bitterness in her voice told him that she did not believe the cow had strayed.

He managed an amused chuckle. "I learned to do without cream. We keep cows on cow ranches to raise beef." He read doubt in her eyes, added with another chuckle, "I'm talking of cattle camps — not the home ranch. Always a few milk cows at the home ranch for milk, cream and butter that never reach a cow camp."

She pulled a chair out opposite him, sat down, watched him dip into the bowl of stew. "I didn't mean to be rude, when you first knocked on the door." She hesitated. "You see, I — I have to be careful."

Hill nodded, took a sip of the hot coffee.

"I don't blame you — alone — like this."

"I'm not usually alone," the girl told him. She was watching him intently. "We're homesteaders, my brother and I ——" The bitterness was back in her voice. "Dick went off yesterday to look for our cow ——" She faltered, and the sudden fear in her grey eyes darkened them to a deep violet. "I'm worried," she finished. "He hasn't come back."

Hill tried to think of a reason. "The storm could have held him up."

"He left early yesterday morning."

"You say you're homesteading this place," Hill continued. "You are new to this country, don't know what cloudbursts can do. Your brother could easily find himself on the wrong side of an arroyo running bank full."

She shook her head. "You are trying to comfort me, Mr. Hill ——" She was suddenly out of her chair, reaching the coffee pot from the stove. The lithe grace of her body as she turned fascinated him. "Plenty of stew in the pot." She filled the mug. Everything about her matched her voice.

He shook his head. "*Gracias,* no ——"

She returned the coffee pot to the stove, resumed her chair, an odd excitement in her eyes as she looked at him. "You speak

Spanish?"

"My grandmother's people were here in New Mexico for some two hundred years before General Kearney marched his troops into Santa Fé. I've been speaking Spanish since cradle days."

The girl's eyes were wide on him. "How — how interesting. I have been taking Spanish for two years," Her smile came — shy, confused under his look. "Well — no reason why I shouldn't explain. Dick has always been wild to come West, to New Mexico. He's not twenty, yet, too young to homestead, so I had to come with him, file on the land in my name. It seemed a good idea to learn Spanish." She broke off, abruptly, gave him an apologetic look. "I'm being so rude, Mr. Hill, talking like this to you and not even telling you who we are. I'm Ellen Dunbar, quite recently from Rhode Island."

Hill crushed the impulse to confess that his full name was Hill Carnady. He said, casually, "You and your brother had a lot of good luck, locating here on Red Butte Springs." He put the empty mug down, shook his head when she reached back for the coffee pot. "Carnady range, isn't it?"

"No luck about it," Ellen Dunbar told him. "I answered an advertisement in a magazine, got in touch with the advertiser, a lawyer in Coldwater."

"I'll make a guess at his name," Hill said. "Oswen Dern."

"Why — yes ——" Her eyes narrowed at him and he saw sudden doubt shadow her face. "He has been very helpful — and kind." Her voice lost its soft melody, took on an edgy note. "You seem to know people in Coldwater, Mr. Hill."

"I told you I had business in Coldwater, Miss Dunbar." Hill's fingers were busy with tobacco and cigarette paper. "Oswen Dern is well known in that town; lawyer, land agent — private banker, and anything else that makes a fast dollar."

"You don't like him?"

"Not too much." Hill put a match to his cigarette. "I must be on my way. You have been very kind to a tired and hungry traveller, Miss Dunbar."

"You don't need to hurry on my account." Her fine eyes clouded. "I'm so worried about Dick, and it's been a relief to talk to somebody."

Hill had no answer for this. He had an uneasy feeling that it was not the storm that delayed Dick's arrival. He leaned back in the stiffly-new rawhide chair, smiled into the troubled eyes opposite him. "Your remark about lamb stew makes me wonder

35

if you plan to run sheep here."

Her face lighted. "We certainly do plan to run sheep. We've taken a government lease on ten thousand acres between here and the river."

Hill said, cautiously, "This has been HC range for a lot of years ——"

Ellen Dunbar interrupted him, her voice almost jubilant. "Oh — that is all settled. I talked it over with old Captain Carnady before I filed the homestead. He was wonderful; told me to go ahead, make a farm here, lease any land not his under deed."

"When was this, Miss Dunbar?" Hill hardly knew the sound of his own voice. "Quite recently?"

She gave him a surprised look. "If you can call six months ago, recently. All this ——" She gestured, a blue print sleeve falling away from slim, rounded arm. "All this was built since Captain Carnady gave me his written agreement."

Hill kept his eyes lowered, fearing she might wonder at the vast relief in his eyes. Whatever the trouble that menaced his grandfather — the old ranch, it had nothing to do with this new little homestead or the young girl sitting opposite him. He said again, "I must be on my way." His look left her, went slowly around the room, every-

36

thing so new, so neat, so clean — breathing the bright courage of this fine, wholesome girl whose young brother was so strangely missing. He got out of his chair, went to the stove, lifted a lid and dropped his cigarette stub into the red coals. He heard her amused laugh.

"Dick drops his anywhere," she said.

"He'll soon learn we don't drop them anywhere," Hill told her. He picked up his still rain-soaked Stetson, stood there, looking at her as she rose from her chair. "Where's that gun you said you had?"

She flushed, shook her head. "I — I was only pretending ——"

He drew the long-barrelled .45 from its holster. "I'll leave mine with you ——"

Her hand lifted in a horrified gesture. "Please — I wouldn't know what to do with it! I've never even held one of those things in my hand."

Hill slid the Colt back into its holster, worriedly rubbed the dark stubble on his chin. He was hating to leave her alone — nobody within ten miles to hear her call for help — if help was needed, her brother mysteriously missing.

She read the indecision in his eyes, gave him a little smile. "I'm not the least bit afraid, Mr. Hill." Her voice sounded oddly breathless to her ears as she looked at the tall man whose weathered young face showed such concern for her. The proud blood of Old Spain, Ellen Dunbar told herself. Conquistador blood from his grandmother whoever she was. The quickened beat of her heart rather startled her. Only a few seconds and this man's face was stamped indelibly in her memory. High nose and cheek bones, the wide, generous mouth that softened their arrogance, the eyes so deep blue in that strong, bronzed face, the quiet voice that spoke of controlled power, authority. Her nerves, so taut with anxiety through the long day, relaxed. She heard a voice — her own voice. "I'm glad I didn't frighten you away with my make-believe gun, Mr. Hill. You'll always be welcome here at Red Butte Springs."

"I'll be back some day," Hill said simply. He crammed the hat on his head, turned to the door, pivoted on boot-heel. "It was the organ that stopped me from passing your gate. The organ — and you — singing that Thanksgiving hymn."

She came quickly to him from the table, a brightness in her eyes. "I know it's a long way from Thanksgiving Day ——" Her face tilted up at him. "We were needing rain so — so dreadfully and I just couldn't help giving thanks."

He rocked back on high heels, thumbs in gun-belt, laughter in his eyes. "Mam — Miss Dunbar, I reckon this whole corner of the Territory is singing a lot of thanksgiving tonight, maybe not the words or the tune you used, but giving thanks, just the same."

Ellen nodded, her smile warm. "I was frightened out of my wits when you came knocking on the door — all alone here and worrying about my brother." Her voice was suddenly not quite steady. "I felt I needn't be afraid when I heard you say you knew that old hymn."

Hill looked at her, concern in his eyes. "I'm hating to go — and your brother not back. You really should have a gun — learn how to use it."

She gave a dubious shake of her head. "I'm afraid I'd never learn ——"

Aware of a disturbing reluctance to leave her, Hill crossed the moonlit yard to the barn. The thirsty earth had already swallowed the little pools of water he had splashed through an hour earlier. His original intention to stay the night until dawn, snatch a few hours' sleep, was no longer feasible. If the brother had been home he would not have hesitated to ask permission to spread his blanket-roll in the barn.

Decency prohibited what might seem like abuse of the girl's hospitality.

He led the refreshed horses from the barn, closed the corral gate and got into his saddle. He was quite sure she would be watching, wondering about the two horses on the lead-rope, perhaps suspicious of his failure to mention them.

He rode slowly along the breast of the slope, eyes alert for the old trail that snaked up from the river road to Comanche Pass — and Coldwater. His uneasiness continued to chafe him as he kept the buckskin moving through the wet, clawing brush. He had the feeling that danger menaced the little homestead at Red Butte Springs. The failure of the girl's brother to return from his chase after the lost cow offered ominous possibilities. *Dick . . . He's not yet twenty. . . .* Hill frowned at the buckskin's alert, pointed ears. Dick's age was not so important. Boys learned self-reliance at an early age in the grim, hard school of the border south-west. But Dick Dunbar was a newcomer from the East — *a tenderfoot.*

The slope levelled into a narrow mesa-like strip. Hill recognized the place — the rock-ribbed cliff, the lone, gnarled piñón tree. *Piñon Mesa.* His boyhood's name for this bit of benchland overlooking the long valley of the San Jacinto.

He drew rein, decision hardening in him. He could not return to the Dunbar Homestead, but he could camp here on the little mesa, keep watch during the night on the Dunbar Homestead. He swung from his saddle, gaze going over his shoulder to the pale gleam of lamplight lower on the slope — almost a mile away. As he watched, the light dimmed out, left only darkness down there.

Slowly, thoughtfully, Hill untied tarp and blanket-roll from the saddle and carried them into the little cave under the cliff. He had slept there a lot of times when he was an adventure-seeking boy before his 'teens. A good dry place even in the worst midsummer rains. He had killed rattlesnakes in that cave, but at this moment he was not thinking of rattlesnakes. He only knew that he had never felt so tired, so dead on his feet for sleep, so longing for a respite from the doubts and fears that had tortured him since the morning Sam Hally's letter had reached him in Denver.

He spread the blankets, returned to the horses, stripped off bridles and saddles and short-tied them to sapling piñons. They had fed well at the Dunbar barn and to put them on ropes to graze was useless in that grass-barren spot.

He turned to the little cave, in haste to fling himself on the blankets, surrender to the sleep that was pulling at his eyes, instead, he forced his attention back to the saddle-gear he had taken from the horses whose riders now lay dead up on the rim-rock. A rifle was in each saddle-boot, blanket-rolls neatly wrapped in tarps.

Hill looked at them thoughtfully. The cave would be a good place to cache these belongings of Topaz and Pedro. No need to take the gear to Coldwater. It was quite possible the slain desperados had friends in Coldwater who would recognize those saddles and carbines.

He looked again down the slope. The Dunbar house was a dim blur under the moon. No light there. *She's gone to bed. . . . Not waiting for Dick.* He picked up the saddles, one in each hand, and carried them into the cave, dropped them on the sand as far back as he could put them in that darkness under the low, arching roof.

He returned to his spread-out blanket, hesitated, stepped outside for another look down the slope at the faint blur in the moonlight that was the Dunbar homestead house. The night was very still. Only the low murmur of the distant San Jacinto — a coyote barking from a nearby hill.

Hill turned wearily into the cave, stretched out on the blanket. He had had a long, heavy day and he made no atempt to fight off the sleep dragging at his eyelids.

CHAPTER THREE

Ellen's face wore a thoughtful look as she cleared the table, poured hot water into a pan from the kettle, washed the dishes and cutlery and put them away. She had watched Hill's departure from the barn, standing at the window of her brother's dark bedroom which overlooked the backyard. His failure to mention the two extra saddle-horses troubled her. It was not the hay he had probably forked into the manger. He was welcome to the hay. What irked her was a growing suspicion that there were gaps in the story of his journey from Santa Fé to Coldwater.

She decided she was letting nerves make her unduly apprehensive. It was entirely possible he had simply forgotten.

She glanced at the clock. *Nearly eleven.* Her thoughts went to Dick. His failure to return from the chase after the cow was alarming, but perhaps Mr. Hill's explanation was reasonable. Dick *could* have been held up by the storm. She tried to take comfort in the thought, picked up the lamp from the table and went into her bedroom. Bed was the best place for her — and sleep. She would need all her strength if something terrible *had* happened to Dick.

Sleep refused to come. The night was so still. Only the coyotes, the hoot of an owl — the distant, muted roar of the river. She could see the moon-bathed cottonwoods beyond her open window. The stillness began to oppress her. She felt frighteningly alone in a vast and hostile world, began to wish she had asked Mr. Hill to stay until morning. He could have slept in the barn. Her restless mind fastened on him. He seemed to know the San Jacinto country — know people in Coldwater, and she had guessed that he did not like Oswen Dern. *Lawyer, land agent — private banker, and anything else that makes a fast dollar.* That was what he had said about Oswen Dern. She wondered drowsily about Mr. Dern, a slender little man with a tiny black moustache carefully waxed at the points, and dark hair, touched with grey at the temples. On the dapper side, in his well-cut Prince Albert, Ellen decided, and trifle too suave. He seemed more like a professional gambler than a respectable lawyer and banker. She had had no valid reason to dislike or mistrust him. He had been courteous enough, and apparently eager to help locate her on a good homestead. She had fallen in love with Red Butte Springs, the big cottonwoods, and the wide expanse of willow brakes down by the creek. His fee of two thousand dollars seemed reasonable. He even offered to see to the filing of the necessary papers that would establish her as lawful owner of the Springs under the Homestead Act, an offer she gratefully accepted when he told her it would save a long trip to Santa Fé.

Ellen closed her eyes. She must stop worrying about Oswen Dern . . . get some sleep . . . silly of her to let Mr. Hill's comment about him upset her.

Her wakefulness persisted and she found herself staring at the moon-splashed cottonwoods beyond the window. It was hard not to worry. The thunderstorm, the rain had taken her mind off Dick for a few minutes. She had felt so happy, so completely thankful for the life-giving rain and couldn't resist the impulse to sit down at the harmonium and sing that Thanksgiving hymn. And now fear was riding her again as midnight approached, and no Dick. Something terrible must have happened to him. He was only nineteen and too young to cope with the dangers of this new and still wild country that was to be their home. He had courage enough, too much courage perhaps, to be cautious.

Again she closed her eyes, tried to go to sleep, counted sheep, pretended they were sheep that would some day be grazing on Red Butte Ranch. That was the name Dick and she had decided on. She counted up to a hundred, putting them one by one through the corral gate. Her wakefulness only increased and her thoughts veered to Oswen Dern, and to Captain Carnady. The old cattleman had given her an odd look when she told him about Oswen Dern's kind offer to register the homestead papers for her in Santa Fé. She recalled his almost gruff comment. *Mighty queer, Dern doesn't seem to know there's a Land Office in Coldwater.* She had failed to grasp his meaning at the time, but learned since that there *was* a Land Office in Coldwater and it would have been easy enough for her to personally register her homestead papers. She had gone to Oswen Dern's office to ask for an explanation, learned that the lawyer was out of town, or supposed to be. She had not been in Coldwater since, or heard from him.

Ellen gazed unhappily at the moonlit night

beyond the bedroom window. It came to her that old Captain Carnady shared her recent visitor's opinion of Oswen Dern. She recalled Hill's laconic answer to her accusation that he did not like the lawyer. *Not too much,* Hill had said.

A coyote began its high, yipping bark, was suddenly silent. Something had frightened it, Ellen decided. She rather liked the little prowlers, or rather she liked to hear their weird howls in the stillness of the night. They were ruthless sheep-killers, she had been warned, and she supposed she would have to make war on them.

She awoke with a start, lay still for a moment, wondering how long she had been asleep, then of a sudden her ears picked up the sound — the soft thud of hoofs in rain-sodden earth. She knew now what had silenced the coyote. Horsemen on the trail, and that meant she had not been asleep more than a few minutes. The coyote had been quite near, perhaps less than a quarter of a mile from the house.

Relief surged through her. Dick! It was Dick coming! She threw back the covers, swung her feet from the bed, pushed them into slippers, sat there on the bed, tense, listening. Her heart sank. Not one horse — several horses. Not Dick — or else he was being brought home, badly hurt — *dead*.

She ran from her room and across the little hall to Dick's bedroom where she could peer through the window that overlooked the back yard. The horsemen were already through the gate — three of them, plainly visible under the bright midnight moon. Three strangers, guns in their belts, rifles in saddle-boots.

Fear constricted her heart. She cowered to one side of the window, continued to watch, hardly daring to breathe. She had never been so frightened, felt so helpless. If only she had urged that nice Mr. Hill to stay. He seemed so competent, so efficient. He would have known what to do with these rough-looking men. She recalled the quiet resolute look of him, realized she must put him out of her thoughts. Thinking of him only made her more acutely aware of her helplessness. It was going to be up to her to rely on her own wits — courage.

The low rumble of voices reached her, gruff, unintelligible words, then a high-pitched voice, a Texan drawl. "Sure, boss. I'll stick with the broncs while you fellers go have your powwow with her."

Ellen heard the creak of saddle leather as the men dismounted, the tread of booted feet approaching the door. She longed wildly for the gun Hill had offered her.

Hard knuckles rapped on the kitchen door. Ellen fled back to her bedroom, pulled on a heavy robe, and hurried into the kitchen.

"Who is it, and what do you want?" She managed to keep her voice steady.

"Bat Savan's the name, ma'am, from HC with a message for you from Cap Carnady."

"It's awfully late to be bringing me a message," Ellen said. "I can't let you in now. I — I'm not dressed."

"It's mighty important, ma'am," insisted the man on the other side of the door.

"Well — why don't you tell me?"

"I reckon you're Miss Dunbar?"

"Of course, and please give me the message."

"Well, ma'am — it's kinder bad news about your brother," answered the gruff voice. "He's back there at the ranch plenty sick. Was fooling with his gun and shot hisself! Showed up at the ranch looking for a stray cow," he added.

Ellen was tearing at the bolt before he had finished. She pulled the door wide open, stood there in the moonlight that flooded through, a hand holding her robe together, her face uplifted in a shocked look at the tall, lanky man standing on the little porch.

"Dick . . . hurt?" Her voice was hardly above a whisper.

"Ain't knowing much how bad," the man told her. He had a dark bony face, and a long upper lip drawn back from discoloured teeth in a grin intended to be reassuring but made Ellen think of a wolf. The man at his heels was moon-faced and chunky with a slit of a mouth and bulging eyes. They made no attempt to remove their big, rain-soaked hats, stood there, eyeing her with an odd mixture of curiosity and sly amusement that she found frightening. She started to close the door. The tall man's grin widened and he reached out a long arm, held the door back and stepped into the kitchen. The chunky man followed. Ellen recoiled, gazed at them helplessly, all colour drained from her face.

The tall man peered around the room. "Git a lamp lit," he said over his shoulder to his companion.

"Kinder dark to see good," complained the moon-faced man. His marble eyes questioned the girl. She pointed mutely at a shelf, and the man slid past her, reached down a small kerosene lamp, placed it on the table and put a match to the wick. "Where do you keep your coal oil?" he asked, not looking at her.

Ellen stared at his broad back, bewildered by the question. It made no sense. Something was terribly wrong. These hard-faced ruffians were not HC men. Old Captain Carnady would scorn to have such scum on his payroll. She heard her voice, fiercely accusing. "You're lying about my brother! And you're *not* from the Carnady ranch!"

The tall man ignored her. "I reckon she keeps her coal oil out in the shed," he said to the other man. "You go git things fixed. Tell Whitey to throw a saddle on a bronc for the gal," he added as his companion hurried to the door. His look went to Ellen. "You git some clothes on, ma'am. We're heading for the ranch."

"You're lying," she repeated. "My brother is — is not at the Carnady ranch." Her voice lacked conviction. She was remembering that the strayed cow was from the Carnady dairy herd, especially chosen for her by the old cattleman himself. It would have been natural for the cow to find its way back to the home pasture.

"Your brother is mighty sick," the man said. "The boss figgers you'll want to see him." His voice hardened. "Go git your clothes on if you want to see him before he cashes in."

His grimace sent a shiver through her. It

was all too plain that further protest was futile. She turned from him, wordless, felt her way down the dark hall to her bedroom, lit the lamp and stood for a moment considering the question of clothes. *Tell Whitey to throw a saddle on a bronc for the gal,* the man had said. She went to the little closet, disregarded the black riding habit she had brought with her from Providence, reached instead for the blue jeans she had learned to use and like despite the conventions that decreed ladies should not ride astride. Side saddles and riding habits had no place in this remote corner of the pioneer southwest.

She pulled them on, tucked in a blue flannel shirt, exchanged her slippers for the soft-leather boots she had bought in Santa Fé, crammed her white Stetson on her dark hair, pocketed a small leather purse that held a few five dollar gold pieces, turned down the lamp wick and thoughtfully watched it flicker out.

Moonlight flowed back into the room as she stood there, thinking of her unpleasant visitors' odd interest in her supply of kerosene. *Where do you keep your coal oil? . . . I reckon she keeps her coal oil out in the shed. . . . You go git things fixed. . . .*

A new and dreadful thought sent cold fingers crawling down her spine. *Coal oil.*

53

Fire. These men were here for a purpose unbelievably evil. She fought for re-assurance, tried to convince herself that she was allowing fear to override sane thinking. She had no enemies — knew nobody who would want to set fire to her little house, burn her new homestead buildings to the ground. It would be such a senseless thing to do. And yet ——

Heavy footsteps sounded in the hall, and Ellen heard the man's voice, harsh — impatient. "Git a move on you, ma'am. Ain't waiting too long ——"

"I'm coming ——" Ellen's look went despairingly around her bedroom. Perhaps she would never see it, or see the little gold-framed miniatures of her father and mother, one on either side of her mirror, now faintly visible in the revealing moonlight. She longed desperately to tear them from the wall, carry them away with her from the doom she intinctively knew was meant for them.

Boot heels pounded up the hall, spurs jingled, and the man was suddenly staring at her from the bedroom door, a gun in his hand.

"Don't be gitting notions," he warned.

Ellen looked at him, and pride put contempt in her eyes, bred coolness in her. She

54

said, quietly, "I have no gun, if that is what's worrying you."

He nodded, slowly holstered the gun. "There won't be no trouble if you come along with us, peaceable."

"You're lying about my brother. I don't believe he's been shot, and I don't believe that Captain Carnady sent any such message."

"How come I knowed your brother ain't here?" argued the man.

Ellen had no answer. It was obvious enough that these men had known that Dick was not home.

"I knowed he wasn't here 'cause I seed him laying back at the ranch, all shot up," continued the man impatiently. "He'll likely be daid before you git to him if you waste time telling me I'm a liar." His voice roughened. "Come on! Let's git moving."

Her look went to the miniatures and suddenly she was reaching them down from their hooks.

"What for you want them pitchers?" asked the man.

Ellen thrust the miniatures into a pocket of the jacket she pulled on over her wool shirt, turned and faced him. "You are here for some wicked purpose." She made the accusation quietly, kept her voice steady. "I have heard of what can happen to unwanted homesteaders, and I know what you plan to do with my cans of coal oil."

The man's hard face creased in his wolf's grin. "The boss ain't liking homesteaders on his cow range," he said. "When he don't like something he gits rid of it, the way he figgers to git rid of this place."

"You fiend!" Hot anger put tears in her eyes, a choke in her voice. "So — so it's all a trick to get me away from here before you burn me out." She was suddenly silent, listening with aghast ears to the sound of gunfire in the back yard — the reverberating reports of a rifle. Her lips mechanically kept count. Four shots. She knew without being told what was happening out there. They were shooting the horses — the wagon team — the buckboard team — killing them in cold blood. And she knew now, the dreadful truth about Dick. They had murdered him, too, her young brother who had come with such hope and courage to make a home in this new country.

The crackle and roar of flames broke through the horror that held her frozen. "No — no!" she cried wildly. She tried to push past the tall shape that blocked the bedroom doorway. His hand fastened on her arm.

"You're some lucky we ain't leaving you

here, too," he said. "We ain't leaving you 'cause the boss says to fetch you back with us."

Ellen looked at him, too dazed to find words. She wondered if she were going to faint, fought off the giddiness and mutely obeyed his gesture to precede him down the hall and through the kitchen. Her knees were like rubber and she almost fell down the porch steps. She was vaguely aware of voices — a great glare from the burning barn. The chunky, moonfaced man hurried past them, disappeared inside the house with a five gallon can of kerosene in his hand. She felt herself pushed towards a cluster of horses near the yard gate. One of them was her own chestnut mare, saddled and bridled. The slight, bow-legged youth holding the mare gave her a sharp look that took her in from head to foot. He had the whitish hair and pale eyes of an albino. She felt she had never seen a more vicious face.

The tall man said, "Give the gal a boost, Whitey. She's kinder droopy seems like."

"Sure, Bat ——" The youth almost lifted her into the saddle. He was amazingly strong for all his slight build. Ellen found herself resenting his unwinking stare. He had the cold, inhuman eyes of a killer and she guessed that it was *his* rifle she had heard. *Whitey.* She mentally catalogued the name. He was the murderer of her horses and she wanted to remember the name of their killer. She sensed that he was the most dangerous of this unsavoury trio.

The tall man whose name was Bat got into his saddle, took the chestnut mare's lead rope in his hand. "You go help Kickapoo git the place to smokin'," he said to Whitey. "I'll take it slow with the gal till you ketch up with us."

They passed through the yard gate and turned into the trail. It seemed to Ellen that all strength had left her. She dropped in the saddle, lifeless, inert, unable to even look back at the flaming horror of the barn where her horses were being turned to cinder. And in a few minutes her little house would be pouring smoke and flame into the midnight sky. Good-bye little homestead — good-bye dreams. One small corner of her dazed mind was tucking away three names. *Bat, Kickapoo — Whitey.* She would remember those names.

She thought of another man. He had told her his name was Hill. She wished she had not let him ride away — leave her so alone — defenceless. This dreadful thing would not have happened if he had stayed.

The mare broke into a slow, ambling trot.

Ellen was tempted to let her limp body tumble from the saddle. She resisted the impulse, clung with both hands to the horn. A fall could only make things worse, perhaps break an arm or a leg. It was up to herself to keep her strength, her wits — her courage — yes, and faith. She was going to need all these things. She closed her eyes, and Bat, glancing back at her, thought she was asleep. Ellen was not asleep, She was asking for help.

CHAPTER FOUR

Something awakened Hill, jerked him upright. He reached hastily for his gun belt, wondering if he had dreamed the gunshot. The next instant he knew it was no dream that had startled him from sleep. The sound shocking his ears was unmistakable in that deep silence of the night, the reverberating report of a rifle.

He was on his feet now, and out of the little cave, buckling on his gun belt, horrified gaze on the red glare less than a mile down the slope. No time to waste trying to understand. He broke into a run towards the little clump of piñons where he had tied the horses, hurriedly got bridle and saddle on the buckskin, took a moment to examine the rifle he had left in its leather scabbard, then surged into the saddle and swung the buckskin in a fast turn. The sharp swerve brushed him against a low-growing piñón that drenched him with still clinging rain drops. The cold shower brought him to his senses. He pulled the horse to a standstill, mopped at his wet face and hair, realized he had forgotten his hat. *Left my brains back with my hat,* he told himself angrily. *Won't help the girl any for me to act like a fool — ride smack into hot lead.*

The night wind came softly from the canyons, brought the sweet smell of damp earth rich with the promise of green grass — wild flowers. He continued to hold his impatience in check while he considered what to do, his gaze fixed on the smoke and flames below. Armed men were down there. They would shoot him out of his saddle at first sight. It was a time for caution — strategy. A dead Hill Carnady would be less than useless to Ellen Dunbar.

Those flames reddening the night meant that somebody was not wanting the Dunbars to homestead Red Butte Springs. And as he sat there on his horse, deciding how he could best help the girl, deliberately cautious now, it came to him that the grim business was tied up with the danger that menaced his grandfather — the ranch. The old cattle man would never have resorted to such ruthless means of warning away an unwanted homesteader. Only one answer was left. A frightening answer. His grandfather was no longer boss of HC. No wonder Sam Hally had written such an urgent letter.

His mind was functioning smoothly again, coolly analysing the situation. He was reasonably sure that the raiders were from HC. He had heard four shots, a significant fact that told the story. These men were there to burn and destroy. They had shot four of the horses. The fifth horse, left alive, would be Ellen Dunbar's chestnut mare which they would need if they planned to take the girl off with them, probably to the ranch. The San Jacinto was running bank full. No chance for them to ford and take the short cut back to the ranch by way of Wild Horse Canyon. The only possible route would be the old river road that dropped down from the Springs and twisted for several miles through dense willow brakes to the wide shallows of Lone Tree Crossing. His one chance to intercept them was down in the brakes, close to the road.

His decision made, Hill rode across to the little cave, got his hat and started down the slope, angling towards the river and keeping to the cover of buckbrush and scrubby piñons and stunted cedars, their wet branches jewelled with moon-glitter.

The little house was burning, adding

smoke and flames to the bonfire of the barn. Perhaps less than ten minutes had passed since the first awakening shot, but fear spurred him. Their mission done, the raiders would lose no time getting away.

He slid from his saddle, tied the buckskin in an alder thicket and ran the remaining ten yards to the roadside. He did not bother to take his rifle. He was familiar with every twist of the road and where he planned to wait it ran like a narrow alley through a dense-growing thicket. His Colt .45 would be best for close, fast action. Ellen Dunbar's safety, perhaps her life, depended on him. He would shoot fast — and shoot to kill. There was no alternative.

He found the place he wanted, a huge-boled Cottonwood tree, its great branches spreading high over the road which was little more than a deep-rutted wagon track. Moonlight lanced through the leaves, threw lattice-work on the wet, dark earth. He pressed close to the rough bark still oozing moisture from the rain, and peered over the crotch of a low limb. Thanks to the moonlight that filtered through the trees he could see where the road made a slow bend from the right; and now his ears picked up the dull thud of approaching hoofs on sodden earth. He waited, tense, gun in hand, eyes straining for anything that moved through those deceptive lights and shadows.

A horseman appeared around the bend, closely followed by a second rider. Ellen Dunbar. Even in that elusive light and despite the fact that she had changed to man's attire, Hill recognized her. He held his breath, keyed his ears for sounds of other riders. Only the hoof thuds of the two horses approaching at a slow jog trot.

They were within ten feet when he stepped into the road, gun lifted, menacing the tall man on the first horse. A rotting branch caught his foot, almost tripped him and in that instant the rider had his gun out. The two shots sounded like one. The desperado's gun slipped from his hand, and dropping the chestnut mare's lead-rope he slumped over saddle-horn, spurred his horse into a dead run. Hill grabbed at the mare's dangling rope, halted her frightened forward plunge, swung her off the road and without a word, led the animal through the brakes to where he had concealed the buckskin in the thicket. Still holding the nervous mare he turned for a first real look at the girl. She seemed very pale in that vague, filtered moonlight. He also saw that her hands were tied to her saddle horn.

Ellen was the first to speak, her voice low,

husky. "I'd given up hope, and then you —— you were suddenly there ——"

He dropped the lead-rope, swiftly freed her wrists from the buckskin thongs. "How many more of them — back there?" he asked.

"Two ——" She began rubbing her chafed wrists and shaking them to restore circulation.

"They'll have heard the shooting. We've got to get away from here — fast," Hill said. He unlooped the reins from the saddle horn. "Can you manage?"

She nodded, took the reins from him. "I'm ready ——"

His head was turned and she saw that he was listening intently. And now she too, heard the distant rataplan of horses on the dead run.

He said, tensely, "Wait! Don't stir from here!" He disappeared, soundless as a stalking Indian. She sat rigid in her saddle, stiff with rising terror, hardly daring to breathe as she listened to the low thunder of those approaching hoof beats. *Where had he gone? What was his purpose in leaving her?*

He was suddenly back. The relief that waved over her left her momentarily limp. His hand lifted in a warning gesture for silence. The approaching riders were around

65

the bend. Kickapoo and Whitey — that appalling *Whitey. Their horses were slowing to a walk.* Ellen's look went despairingly to the tall man standing close to her. No fear showed on that dark-stubbled face. Only resolute purpose — alert readiness. For some reason her rising panic subsided.

Voices reached them from the road, Kickapoo's surly grumble — Whitey's nasal whine. "Sure heard shooting," the latter declared. "And right now I got me a notion I'm smelling gunsmoke hereabouts."

"I reckon Bat took a shot at a coyote," Kickapoo surmised.

"Mebbe the gal took a shot at him," suggested Whitey. "Mebbe she hid his body in the brakes here some place and got to hell away from here fast."

"You're talking *loco,*" grumbled the other man. "She wasn't carrying a gun, and her hands were tied to the saddle. Come on, feller. Quit looking for trouble where there ain't any."

"She's sure one honey." Whitey's high cackle sent a shiver through Ellen. "I crave to git real acquainted with that gal."

The voices faded into the distance. Hill relaxed, turned and gave the girl a faint smile. "It's lucky I remembered the gun he dropped," he said.

Ellen glanced at the guns he held in either hand. One of them was the gun Bat had dropped when he spurred away. "Not luck," she demurred. "It was fast thinking. They might have seen it lying there — known it wasn't a coyote."

His face hardened again. "We've got to get away from here in a hurry. They may run into a dead man — up the road." He holstered his own .45, thrust the other into the leather scabbard that held his rifle, untied his horse and got into his saddle.

No words passed between them as they rode out of the brakes and turned their horses up the slope. Hill looked back only once at the girl closely following his twisting course through the piñons. They reached the little cave under the great cliff.

Ellen broke the silence. "You camped here, after you left me." It was a statement rather than a question.

Hill said ruefully, "I shouldn't have left you — and your brother not back." He slid from his saddle. "I'll get my gear, and then we'll keep moving." He hurried into the cave, reappeared, dragging his tarp on which lay his blanket and slicker. He quickly made a neat roll, fastened it on his saddle. His look went thoughtfully to the two horses tied in the piñons. He was tempted to turn them loose, let them find their way back to the ranch. The news would be out that somebody had witnessed the raid on the Dunbar homestead. One of the raiders was either dead or badly wounded — the girl gone. They would suspect Hill Carnady, realize he had escaped the ambush laid for him on the rimrock.

He checked the impulse. It was better to leave them in the dark as long as possible about the fate that had overtaken Topaz and Pedro. They could not be sure that Hill Carnady had escaped their hired killers. Let them puzzle for a while about Topaz and Pedro, and the mysterious attack that had rescued Ellen Dunbar from the raiders.

His decision made, Hill untied the horses, put them on a lead-rope and got into his saddle.

Ellen was gazing unhappily down the slope at the burning buildings. "I can't believe it," she said, half to herself. "I — I'm dreaming ——" She heard Hill's voice, terse, urgent, tore her look from the red glow down the hill and reined her mare alongside his buckskin.

They rode side by side across the little mesa, the two horses trailing on the lead-rope. Hill said, "It's a good ten miles to Coldwater . . . rough country — some of it." He glanced over his shoulder at the moon. "Nearly two o'clock. We should make it by sunrise — with luck."

Ellen, looked at the red glow over the Springs. "It seems hours and hours — since those — those beasts rode into the yard," she said, dejectedly.

"Who were they?" Hill almost dreaded the answer to his question.

"They tricked me — said they had a message from Captain Carnady." She paused, wondering at the stark agony in his eyes as he looked at her. "They said Dick had been accidentally shot and was dying and that Captain Carnady had sent them for me." Her voice choked and she halted the mare. "I think I'm going to cry," she said. "Please go on — don't look at me."

Hill rode on a few yards, pulled to a standstill. He had never felt such heart-sickness, felt so useless.

She drew up alongside presently, gave him a faint, wet-eyed smile, and they rode on, left the mesa and turned up a hillside trail wide enough for the two of them to ride abreast, but showing signs of long disuse. It was higher country here, and pines began to show, and mountain mahogany. The soft wind whispered out of some nearby canyon, cool, refreshing. Ellen could no longer see the smoke and flames of the burning home-stead.

She gave her tall companion a curious look. "You seem to know your way over these hills."

"I was born here — in this country," admitted Hill. He paused, "Tell me all that happened, Miss Dunbar. You see — they probably lied about your brother — and anyway, I want to help."

"It's all so mysterious," Ellen said. "I can't believe that Captain Carnady sent those men to burn us out. He seemed so fine — kind."

"I've known him a long time — all my life," Hill said. "They don't come finer than Captain Carnady."

"You know him?" exclaimed Ellen. She halted the mare, surprise on her upturned face. "You didn't tell me that you knew him, Mr. Hill."

Hill waited for her to come alongside again. "I wasn't sure how you'd take it. You see, I'm his grandson — Hill Carnady."

"Then you must have known all about Dick and me homesteading the Springs." Her tone was vexed, tinged with suspicion.

Hill shook his head. "I've been away for a year at the Denver School of Mines. All I know is that something is terribly wrong at the ranch."

Ellen halted the mare again. "I think you should tell me why you think something is wrong at the ranch. I can only guess — because of what happened tonight."

Hill said, "We've got to keep moving. Those men will likely be looking for us."

CHAPTER FIVE

They forded a small creek, brawly with storm waters, and the trail narrowed, pitched down a rocky hillside. Hill took the lead, and Ellen was forced to follow the two horses he had on the lead-rope. The moon was at their backs, and she saw a great red star lifting above the dark wall of the mountains ahead. *Mars,* she guessed.

They were presently on level ground again, and the trail wide enough for her to put the mare alongside the buckskin. Hill gave her an encouraging smile.

"I don't blame you for wondering about me," he said. "I was wondering about you, too, when I rode up from the creek and saw lamplight winking from Red Butte Springs. I had been warned to look out for trouble. I wouldn't have dared to stop if I hadn't heard you singing that Thanksgiving hymn."

"I was so happy," Ellen said and she added with a shudder, "It's been a horrible nightmare ever since." Her face lifted in a troubled look at him. "Why would you have been afraid to stop?"

He told her about Sam Hally's letter — the attempt to ambush him on the rimrock. "They were riding these horses I'm taking to Coldwater. *HC horses,*" he emphasized. "The fact that they were watching for me indicates that Sam Hally had good reason to suspect that my grandfather is in great danger. He wouldn't have had killers like Topaz and Pedro on his payroll."

"I had the same feeling about the men who came tonight," Ellen said. "I just knew that Captain Carnady wouldn't have such scum in his employ. I told them so," she added fiercely. "I told them I didn't believe for a moment that Captain Carnady had sent them with any such message about my brother." She paused, added perplexedly, "I still don't understand why you thought it might be unsafe to stop at our house."

"There was no house at the Springs when I left the ranch a year ago," Hill explained. "I didn't know what to make of it when I saw your lamplight. It was possible that whoever was living there might be involved in the attempt to ambush me." He gave her a grin. "I knew different when I heard you singing."

"I thought it was Dick — your step," Ellen said. "Your knock warned me it was not
Dick. He'd have yelled for me to open when
he found the door locked." She faltered.
"I'm dreadfully worried about him."

"Those men *could* have been lying," Hill
tried to comfort.

Ellen shook her head. "The one who
called himself Bat knew about our lost cow.
He couldn't have known unless Dick had
been at the ranch." Her face lifted in a worried look. "You see — your grandfather *gave*
us that cow, said she was the best milker in
the Territory of New Mexico."

"Brown Bess," chuckled Hill. "Seven gal-
lons a day."

Ellen nodded. "That's her name. Captain
Carnady wouldn't let us pay a penny for
her, insisted she was his present to the new
homestead."

"It proves that he couldn't have had
anything to do with what has just happened
to the homestead," Hill said with conviction.

"Of course it does!" she declared vehe-
mently. "My heart tells me he has nothing
to do with it."

Hill reached out, gave her hand a little
squeeze; and they jogged on through the
moonlit stillness. Only the muted thud of

hoofs in wet earth, the flinty strike of horseshoes on rain-washed granite. The trail narrowed again and Ellen dropped back to follow the two horses on the lead-rope. She had wanted to talk, ask him questions, but more talk was impossible until the trail widened. She wondered if he would recognize the names of the men who had burned the homestead and attempted to carry her away. *Bat — Kickapoo, Whitey.* She felt that she could never forget those names. To think of them sent cold prickles through her. They stood for sheer horror. She wondered why they had wanted to take her to the ranch. Bat had told her that Dick had sent for her because he was dying. She might have believed him at first, but not after what they had done to the homestead. It numbed her to think about Dick. *He's dead — murdered.* Hill's voice dragged her from terrifying thoughts.

"Steep climb here," he called. "Take it easy, and watch out for loose shale."

She held the mare back, heard the scramble of shod hoofs ahead, the rattle of small stones — the snorts of horses. The mare went up slowly, feeling her way cautiously over slippery shale. Tall cliffs lifted on either side, shut out the moonlight, and the trail continued up in sharp, frightening

75

loops that held her tense in the saddle. She heard Hill's encouraging voice floating down to her; and suddenly the cliffs drew apart and she saw him waiting for her at the edge of a small meadow rimmed by the shadowing cliffs.

"Comanche Pass," Hill said. "We're over the hump." He gestured across the little meadow to where a dark gap broke the encircling high cliff. "A bit steep in places, going down the canyon."

"Is it a long way, yet, to Coldwater?" she asked.

The weariness in her voice drew a sharp look from him. "We can rest for a few minutes if you're getting too tired."

She shook her head, "No, no! I can make it ——"

"Another two hours," Hill told her.

"Those men," Ellen reminded. "They might be following us." She straightened determinedly in the saddle. "Come on! The thought of them frightens me."

He gave her a relieved look and they rode over to the gap where the canyon began its downward plunge. Ellen got an impression of a dark, forbidding chasm that apparently had no bottom. The trail went down gently at first, twisting around tumbled boulders. A wide bend pointed them almost due west, and far below them lay the long valley of the Coldwater, a misty silver sea under the moon now reaching low to the opposite peaks.

At times where the trail permitted, they rode stirrup to stirrup, talking little, but thinking much. Ellen asked one direct question. Would the names of Bat, Kickapoo, and Whitey mean anything to Hill? He answered tersely that he had never heard of them. She saw that his mind was seething with the same torturing fears that assailed her and refrained from further questions.

The murmur of a stream began to touch her ears as the looping trail dropped them lower and lower. Comanche Creek, Hill informed her, rushing its storm waters to the Coldwater River.

At last they were down on the flats. Hill took a hasty backward look up the rugged slopes. The moon, now poised like a great silver disc over the mountains beyond the valley, touched a hairpin turn a thousand feet above him, and he fancied he glimpsed a dark moving shape up there. A lone rider, and that meant pursuit.

All he said to the girl was, "We can move fast, now." And he put the buckskin to an easy lope. Her mare rocked alongside at a fast, smooth running walk that drew his attention.

He said, surprise in his voice, "That's a Tennessee horse!"

"Captain Carnady gave her to me," Ellen told him. "He said she would be as easy as a rocking chair — and she is."

"I thought I recognized her. Haven't really looked at her until just now." Hill's tone was thoughtful. Another nail clinching the evidence that his grandfather was not responsible for the wanton raid on the Dunbar homestead. Also dreadful proof that the kindly old cowman was either dead or the helpless victim of some sinister plot to gain possession of the ranch.

The same thought was in Ellen's mind, and her face lifted in an earnest look at him. "I just knew that he *couldn't* have done this to Dick and me." Her smile came, quick, warm — comforting.

The moon was down behind the mountains when they reached the outskirts of Coldwater and they rode through the darkness that precedes the first flush of early dawn. The little cow town had not yet come awake, which was what Hill wanted and hoped for. To be seen by curious eyes was an invitation to danger.

He had already decided on the one safe

place for Ellen Dunbar. And it was there that he would be most likely to find either Sam Hally or Seth McGee. Sam Hally had promised that one of them would be waiting for him in Coldwater, and with Sam a promise was a promise.

They crossed the stage road that swooped on them from around a great butte. Hill glanced up the little town's main street, saw with relief that no life stirred there. Another three minutes brought them to an ancient, flat-roofed adobe overlooking a creek that twisted down from the hills back of the town. A long-legged sow was rooting for fallen fruit under a huge fig tree. She took a surprised look at the approaching riders, grunted wrathfully at the intrusion and scurried away. A man's voice spoke from behind the closed door.

"*Quién es?*"

"Quick!" Hill called softly in Spanish. "Open up, Pablo!"

A gnarled brown face with a drooping, grizzled moustache, peered out, and suddenly the door opened wide, framed the owner of the face. "*Por Dios!* It is you, *Señor!*" He shook his grey head worriedly. "It is dangerous for you here. Bad men in this town seek your life." He came up close, surprise widening his eyes as he saw that

79

Hill's companion was a girl. "*Señor* — go before it is too late!"

Hill interrupted him. "Tell me — is Don Julio home?"

"*Sí.*" Pablo nodded.

"You tell him I coming in from the creek side," Hill instructed. "I'll want somebody to let us in at the back gate."

"*Sí,*" promised the Mexican. "I will tell him."

"I think we've been followed over Comanche Pass," Hill continued. Ellen's exclamation interrupted him.

"You didn't tell me!" She paused, added thoughtfully, "If you're right — it will be that horrible Whitey." Her look went to Pablo. "He is young and skinny and has pale blue eyes and almost white hair — an albino."

"I 'ave know thees Whitey," the Mexican told her. "Ver bad hombre."

"Tell him you haven't seen us, if he asks you," Hill said, in Spanish. He looked over at the creek. "We'll take to the water, Pablo — ride up the creek. We won't be leaving any trail to Don Julio."

"It is a good idea," agreed the old Mexican. "The flood has passed and the creek will soon be dry again unless more rain comes."

A pale glow was warming the eastern peaks when Hill and Ellen left the shallow waters of the creek and rode some hundred yards to the massive gate set in a twelve foot adobe wall reared between two lofty red buttes that made Ellen think of giant watchtowers rising above the bastions of some ancient fortress. She was surprised to find that there was more truth than fiction in her passing thought. A voice challenged them from the summit of one of the buttes.

"Quién es?"

Ellen's heart quickened as her upward look discovered the challenger, distinctly visible in the growing light. She was aware of a steeple hat, a rifle, levelled at them. She heard Hill speak laconic Spanish words.

"Hill Carnady, to see Don Julio."

"*El Señor* comes now," said another voice from the opposite butte.

The two steeple-hatted sentries were suddenly up from their crouch; rifle butts struck stone, two voices spoke in unison. "A thousand pardons, *Señor.*"

"The light was poor," said the man who had challenged them.

"You are forgiven, Atilano," Hill assured him.

"I should have known you among ten thousand," groaned the other sentry.

"Do not think of the matter again, Justo," Hill said. He gave the wondering girl on the chestnut mare an amused grin.

Footsteps rapidly approached the other side of the gate. From the clatter they made, Ellen visualized worn adobe paving blocks; she heard a harsh, rather high-pitched voice, an imperative voice, accustomed to long years of command, and now touched with the irascibility of advanced age. Her Spanish was limited, but she could vaguely understand.

Heavy iron bars and chains clanked and rattled, the great iron-strapped gate creaked open, and she saw a tall, fiercely-erect man with close-cropped stiff white hair, a bristling white moustache and short beard. The dark eyes under beetling brows were hot with excitement. The long robe of heavy red silk indicated that he had just been routed from his bed. Several men were at his back, all of them armed.

His arms opened wide, *"Hillito!"* Emotion shook his voice. "I had not hoped to ever see you in the flesh again!"

Hill and Ellen rode into the great yard with the two led horses. Hill slid from his saddle, reached out a hand to help the girl from her saddle. She was stiff from the long, punishing ride, felt awkward, clinging to

Hill's hand and facing this imperious old hidalgo. To her dazed mind he and his establishment did not belong on the American side of the border. She had the feeling that she was looking at a picture page torn from a history of Old Mexico.

She heard Hill's voice, introducing the hidalgo to her. "Señor Julio Severa," Hill said. His hand tightened over hers in a reassuring clasp as though he sensed her confused state of mind. "My great-uncle," Hill said, speaking in English. "My grandmother's only brother and the last of his name."

Don Julio returned her wan smile with a stiff little bow. She felt dreadfully tired, physically and mentally, managed to make sense of the Spanish words Hill was saying to his great-uncle. "Miss Ellen Dunbar," he introduced. "My very dear friend."

Don Julio bowed again; a smile showed long, yellow teeth through bearded lips. "I welcome the Señorita Dunbar," he said, speaking in careful English. "My house is hers as long as she cares to honour it with her charming presence." His look returned almost immediately to Hill. "My dear boy ——" Worry gravelled his voice. "I fear you are in great trouble — and the young señorita ——"

"She needs your protection," Hill said, bluntly. "She is in great danger."

Ellen felt the battery of Don Julio's hot eyes studying her intently for a moment. His voice lifted, a harsh, rasping bark. "Justo — Atilano! Down here." He spoke more words to the men grouped at his back. One of them led the four horses away, two others ran hastily to occupy the lookout posts being vacated by Justo and Atilano, Don Julio in the meantime listening intently, a deepening frown on his brow, to low-voiced words from Hill.

Justo and Atilano appeared, erect, compactly-built, swarthy, impassive. Yaquis, Ellen guessed; and to her surprise she saw that they were twins. They were like two peas in a pod.

Don Julio turned fierce eyes on them, gestured at the girl. "Guard her with your lives," he commanded.

"Si, Señor," they said in unison.

"Swear on your oath," rasped the old hidalgo. "Day and night you will guard the young señorita."

The twins crossed thumbs over forefingers. *"Por esta cruz,"* they muttered like one voice. "With our lives, *Señor.*"

"Come," Don Julio said. "We will go to the house." For the first time a real smile animated his gaunt face, warmed his eyes as he looked at the weary girl whose hand Hill still held. "Señorita Dunbar need rest — and then good food to restore her strength."

Hill lifted a hand, an urgent gesture. "Please, my dear uncle! Tell me — is Sam Hally here, or Seth McGee?"

Don Julio shook his head an odd glint in his heavy-lidded eyes. "Señor McGee has disappeared," he said, slowly, almost reluctantly. "Your friend, Señor Hally is now in the *carcel,* accused of attempted murder." He hesitated, worry on his face. "There is talk of a — a lynching ——"

Ellen knew enough Spanish to get the drift of the old Mexican's words. She quite understood the reason for the bewilderment, the horror, that spread over Hill's face. He was like a man who had been struck a mortal blow. She freed her hand from his hard clasp, slipped her arm under his. "We won't let them," she said. "We won't let them do *that* to him, Hill!"

CHAPTER SIX

The freight wagons drew slowly up the
street now already baked dry under the hot
July sun. The shod hoofs of the ten-mule
hitch, the grind of ponderous wheels, lifted
a thin haze of dust that drifted lazily in the
lifeless noonday air. The freighter, swaying
easily to the motion of the big wheeler he
rode, looked curiously at the girl on the
porch of the Coldwater Palace Hotel. His
Mexican swamper, perched on the high seat
of the rear wagon, turned his dark face in a
similar interested stare. They were hardened
to the perils of the long haul between Silver
City and Albuquerque — cloudbursts, dry
water-holes, Indians; but a girl wearing the
pants of a man was something else.

Their undisguised amazement seemed to
amuse the girl. Her hand lifted in a friendly
wave that brought no response from the
teamster. He spat a dark-brown stream over
the ear of his wheeler, spoke gruff words

that made the mules lunge into their collars. His swamper was more polite, sent back a white-toothed smile. He was wondering what his beloved Maria Concepción would say to his story of this gringo señorita. *Verdad!* Maria Concepción would say he had been imbibing too much vile gringo whisky.

A man pushed through the screen door of the lobby, stood for a moment, a hint of laughter in his eyes as he took in the scene. He was tall, of middle age, with the weathered face of an outdoors man and a touch of grey in his hair. He wore a battered wide-brimmed hat and a brown linen shirt and work-stained corduroys tucked into brush-scarred boots.

"I'm afraid you've given the natives a shock, Lucy," he said with a chuckle. "And where in the name of Mother Grundy did you get that outfit you're wearing?"

The girl turned her head in a look at him. The hair under her white Stetson was dark and she wore a blue flannel shirt and blue levis tucked into soft-leather boots. "Oh, Dad!" she exclaimed. "I simply *must* paint that!" She gestured at the freight wagons, tilted her head in a critical study of the distant red butte where the stage road made its bend beyond the town. "Over there, with that big red rock for a background. All those colours — the bits of fleecy clouds in that blue sky."

"You haven't answered my question," reminded Dr. Homer Royale. He drew pipe and pouch from a pocket, tamped in tobacco. "What's the idea?"

"You mean these things?" Lucy glanced down at her blue-jeaned legs. "Why — I bought them this morning, while you were writing up your notes about your old rocks and things." Her gesture indicated a building across the street where a sign painted on the false front advertised Coldwater's *General Merchandise Store, Jake Kurtz, Prop.* "Such a fascinating place, Dad! And the nicest old German store-keeper. It's the only store for miles and miles and he keeps everything under the sun" — she gave him an impish grin — "including Stetson hats and the trousers favoured by gentlemen of the western cow country."

Her father's heavy brows drew down in a mock frown. "I thought I was bringing you up to be a lady ——"

"I'm not going to sit here while you and Bill Wallace go poking around in your old canyons, chipping rocks with your hammers," Lucy declared. "I'm going to do some *painting* while you look for your hidden gold and silver and whatever." She gave her jean-clad legs a complacent look. "Such a wonderful country to paint, but no place for a girl in skirts with its cactus and clawing brush and rocks and rattlesnakes — and everything. I'm only being practical, Daddy, dear."

"Practical," agreed Dr. Royale; "also somewhat ahead of your time, but yes, practical."

"I'm not the first," Lucy told him. "That nice old Mr. Kurtz in the store said he'd sold exactly the same outfit to another girl quite recently. He wasn't the least surprised — asked me if we were sisters. We looked alike, he said, and wore the same size, and ____"

The slam of the screen door interrupted her. She smiled up at the man who joined them. He was young, rugged in build and face, a blond, blue-eyed viking, and like her father, wearing clothes that had seen a lot of the rough outdoors.

"Sorry to keep you waiting, Chief," he said to Lucy's father. "Took longer than I expected to work out those figures you gave me." He broke off, widened his eyes at the girl who wagged a finger at him.

"Not a word from you, Bill Wallace. I'm only using good common sense, even if

89

father *does* say I'm somewhat ahead of my time."

The young man's sunburned face took on a deeper tinge; he choked off an exclamation, grinned at her. "There's only one word, I can say, Lucy." There was a touch of the Scot in his voice. "Bonny is the word; aye, a bonny lassie you are in — in ——" He floundered, handed her a small canvas-covered box. "Brought your paint things down," he finished.

"You'll have to get used to them," Lucy said with a complacent glance at her jeans. Her look went to the buckboard approaching up the street from the livery barn. "Well, on your way, boys. Have a good time with your rocks and things."

"Aren't you coming with us?" queried her father as the buckboard drew up in front of the hotel.

Lucy shook her head. "I've ordered a horse," she told them. "I'm going sketching with my little kit." She glanced up the street at the dust-veiled freight wagons. "No chance there, now," she mourned. Her look shifted to the small plaza lower down the street, the crumbled adobe walls of the ancient church. "I must do that old mission church before we leave Coldwater. Poor old ruin." She shook her head. "I've an idea they could do with a church in this town."

"Coldwater is an old pueblo," her father said. "Settled by the Franciscan padres long before Kearney's troops entered Santa Fé. They called the place *Agua Frio* because of the always flowing cold springs. The population is still more than eighty per cent Mexican." He gazed thoughtfully at the grey old walls. "We gringos have not done much good here, but I've an idea the great doors of that old church are still open for saint or sinner."

"Father!" Lucy Royale reached hastily for her painting kit. "Those two Mexicans coming from the plaza! Give me some silver. I *must* get a sketch of them."

The two Mexicans crossed the street and approached up the planked sidewalk. They wore tall steeple hats of plaited straw, brush-scarred leather chaps and bright-coloured serapes slung over shoulders.

"Vaqueros," pronounced Lucy's father. He handed her a couple of coins.

Lucy beckoned to them, showed the silver coins in her hand. "Please," she called, "I want to sketch you." She gestured at the ancient hitch-rail in front of the hotel. "Lean against those old posts for a few minutes and make cigarettes or something."

The taller of the two flashed her a startled

look, quickly hid his face behind his serape. His grizzled-haired companion shook his head.

"We beeg 'urry, Señorita ——" His pace quickened to overtake the younger man's lengthened stride.

Lucy's chagrined gaze followed them for a moment. Her head turned in a wondering look at her father. "He has blue eyes," she marvelled. "That tall young Mexican's eyes were as blue as the sky."

"Conquistador blood in him," guessed Dr. Royale.

"And red in his hair," Lucy said. She stood there, a hint of a frown in her own grey eyes. "He didn't want us to see his face," she added in a puzzled voice.

"The poor fellow got bashful," chuckled Bill Wallace. "Probably the first time he's seen a woman dressed like a man." He followed her father down the steps and the two men climbed into the buckboard's back seat.

"Stop at Oswen Dern's office," Dr. Royale told the driver. The man nodded, drove a few doors up the street and halted the team in front of an obviously new one storey frame building glistening with a coat of white paint. Gold-leaf letters on the single window said, *Oswen Dern. Attorney at Law.*

Land Agent. Dr. Royale started to get out. The driver turned an unshaven, sunburned face in a look at him.

"He ain't in," he said. "Card on the door says he won't be back till three o'clock."

The geologist grunted, settled back in the seat. "No sense waiting for him," he said to his assistant. He stared thoughtfully at the driver's thick, red neck. "Do you know the road to Red Butte Springs?" he asked.

"Sure do."

"What's your name?"

The driver shifted his tobacco quid, spat over a wheel. "Piute'll do," he answered laconically.

"All right, Piute," Dr. Royale put a match to his pipe. "Head for this Red Butte place. Dern is anxious for an opinion . . . thinks there is gold there," he said in a lowered voice to Bill Wallace.

Piute swung the team and they drove past the hotel, dust trailing the spinning wheels. Lucy was talking to a man who was tying her paint kit to the saddle of the horse he had brought from the livery barn. She threw a jaunty wave at them.

Bill Wallace waved back at her, said in a worried voice, "You shouldn't let her go riding off alone, Chief."

"No danger of her getting lost," rejoined

93

Dr. Royale. "Lucy is used to roaming around by herself."

"An awful lot of country here," grumbled the young Scot. "And getting lost isn't the *only* danger."

Lucy got into her saddle, rode up the street and turned into the stage road that swooped around the great lone butte. She wanted to overtake the lumbering freight outfit, perhaps succeed in persuading the hard-eyed teamster to let her get a sketch with the butte as a background. There were some nice fluffy clouds pushing over the distant mountain peaks, too. Just what she needed to bring out that wonderful blue of the sky.

She caught a glimpse of the two Mexicans who had been too *beeg 'urry* for her to sketch them. They were leisurely climbing a short, dusty road towards a squat adobe building half hidden in a grove of ancient cottonwood trees. They did not seem in such haste, now, she reflected with some indignation. Curious about that younger Mexican's blue eyes and decidedly red hair. Handsome, too. A fine, strong face. She could have made something out of him.

Coldwater's little main street was coming to life after the noonday *siesta*. Men appeared from the several saloons, grouped

94

on the sidewalk, some of them moving off towards the livery barn at the end of the street, high heels clattering on the rough board walk. A light ranch wagon halted in front of the livery barn and a sun-bonnetted woman climbed down from the seat, spoke to the driver, evidently her husband, and hurried towards the store opposite the hotel. The man swung his team into the big livery yard. Some half score riders headed by a tall, lean man with a hawk's face and handle-bar black moustache, drifted up the street, turned into the same livery yard. One of the saloon sidewalk loafers spoke to his companion.

"Looks like your HC outfit's in town, Whitey."

Whitey was staring up the street, gaze fastened on the girl at that moment disappearing around the lone butte. His pale eyes had an exulting gleam in them; he said in his high, nasal voice, "Ain't wanting Jess Kinner to know I'm in town, Kansas. Keep your mouth shut, or you'll be damn sorry."

Kansas, bow-legged, hard-faced, gave him an outraged look. "I ain't carin' enough for your HC outfit to tell 'em you're in town."

"I got bus'ness to 'tend to," Whitey explained. "Just as quick as I can sneak back to the barn and git my bronc without Jess

95

or the boys spotting me, I'm riding away from here."

"To hell with you and HC," Kansas said. He pushed back through the swing doors, sauntered through the long saloon to a rear door and vanished in the brush beyond. He had even more urgent reasons than Whitey for not wanting to be seen by HC's foreman.

Whitey, after a furtive glance up and down the street, broke into the quick, choppy run of a cowboy on high heels, squeezed from view in the narrow gap between the saloon and the adjoining barber shop.

Hill Carnady, too had glimpsed Lucy Royale when she rode across the dusty road he was climbing with Pablo Sanchez. His first look at her when passing the Palace Hotel had startled him almost out of his wits. Her voice, asking them to pose for her against the hitch-rail had instantly told him that she was *not* Ellen Dunbar, despite the blue levis, the blue flannel shirt — the white Stetson, a garb that made them look astonishingly alike. Also he knew that Ellen Dunbar was safely hidden behind Don Julio Severa's high adobe walls. Instinctively he had concealed his face, nudged Pablo to deny the unknown girl's request.

He was on a desperate venture. Life or

death lay in the balance. It was not much that Don Julio had been able to tell him, only that the little cowtown of Coldwater was in the grip of wicked gringos, and that immediate action alone could save old Sam Hally from dangling at the end of a rope before the sun again lifted above the mountains.

Of his long-dead sister's husband, Captain Carnady, Don Julio had no news. It was his belief that Hill's grandfather was dead. It was because of trying to help Captain Carnady that Seth McGee had mysteriously disappeared, and Sam Hally threatened with the unhappy and imminent prospect of dancing on air at the end of a lynch mob's rope. There was nothing, Don Julio sadly confessed, that he could do about it, except withdraw behind the well-guarded walls of his *casa,* trust to the vigilance of his score or more retainers, and the prayers of the old padre who still defied the *malo* gringos from the sanctuary of the ancient plaza church.

It was at this point in his narrative that Don Julio's sonorous voice had choked and his sunken eyes became suspiciously bright. "Your appearance with the rising of the sun is an answer to our good Padre Francisco's prayers," he declared. "You bring me hope, grandson of my dear sister Isabel!"

Small hope, Hill thought unhappily, as he slowed his stride up the hill towards the low squat adobe building that was Coldwater's jail. He must hold impatience in check, make it seem to chance eyes that they were only two Mexican *peones* with nothing to do, nowhere to go — just wandering up the hill.

"Take it easy," he warned Pablo Sanchez. "Haste can attract attention."

"Si, Señor," muttered Pablo. He continued in Spanish, "The little señorita who spoke to us was our little señorita, no?" His tone was puzzled. "She looked the same, but her voice — it was not the same."

"She was *not* our señorita, who is now under the watchful eyes of Justo and Atilano," reassured Hill.

"I was frightened." Pablo's finger, gnarled as bits of sun-dried mesquite, swiftly shaped the Cross on his breast. "I could have sworn it was our señorita."

Hill hardly heard him. His thoughts were on the immediate problem confronting him. There had been short time to think. The situation demanded action, fast, furious action that would save old Sam Hally. He was like a man treading a narrow trail. A wrong step to right or left could plunge him down

98

a precipice — to oblivion. His talk with Don Julio had convinced him that only one thing could save Sam Hally — boldness — a surprise attack. Caution — yes, against the wrong step; but boldness so daring that surprise would win victory. He had thought the plan out from every angle, even to this very hour that found him climbing up to Coldwater's ancient jail with loyal old Pablo at his side. He silently applauded the aged Mexican's courage. Pablo quite understood what could happen to him if the plan failed. Pablo was old, but loyalty and courage still fired the blood in him.

He heard the old man's voice, soft-spoken. "The *carcel, Señor* — and — we are alone, near the door." Pablo's look went over his shoulder. "Dust down there," he said, his voice a low, worried growl. "They come, *Señor* — the men who wish to hang our good Señor Hally."

"Slow those feet of yours," muttered Hill. He began to shape a brown-paper cigarette, rolled his eyes in pretended amusement at Pablo. "Eyes may be watching us from the *carcel,*" he warned. "Remember to do what I said."

"*Si, Señor* ——" Pablo came to a standstill, pushed at his steeple hat, burst into crack-voiced song. He staggered, leaned heavily against Hill. *"Por Dios!"* His voice was loud, drunken. "I dreenk too mooch red vino, no, Juan Escobar?"

"Peeg!" shouted Hill. He gave his companion an indignant shove. "We come for see poor Juanito and you go dreenk the red vino. Loco!"

The jail door opened, framed a red-jowled man, legs wide apart, fat stomach slopping over his gun-belt. The gun was menacing in uplifted hand. "What brings you Mex hombres up here?" he asked. His voice was drink-thickened, truculent. "Answer quick, or I'm squeezin' trigger ——"

Hill had hardly dared hope for a chance so favourable to his plan to reach Sam Hally. A *loco* plan, old Don Julio had gloomily told him. Yet no other means could have brought him through Coldwater's main street, up the hill to the jail. His vaquero clothes, steeple hat, serape — chaps, and old Pablo Sanchez. To have shown himself as Hill Carnady would have meant instant disaster, a quick bullet. He was sure of that, now. He had dared the risk, and only one pair of eyes had seen under the mask of his vaquero garb, the lovely eyes of the girl on the hotel porch. So amazingly like Ellen Dunbar's eyes; and her startled look had warned him that she suspected he

100

was not what he seemed to be.

He heard Pablo going into his well-drilled act, voice quavering, properly drunken. "Señor Pinto — we breeng leetle *mescal* for my Juanito."

"Huh?" The jailer's blood-shot eyes narrowed greedily. *"Mescal?"*

"Si, Señor ——"

"We're hangin' that Mex for pulling his knife on the marshal. This town ain' standing for you Mex fellers talking back to us, and that's why we're swinging Juanito, Savvy?"

"Si, Señor." Pablo drew a flask from a pocket under his serape. "Juanito like nize dreenk w'en sweeng, no?"

"Mescal, huh?" Pinto snatched the flask from Pablo's hand, held it close to bleary eyes. "Looks like the real stuff, Pablo, and I sure ain't wasting it on no damn Mex that's due to swing."

"Señor!" protested Pablo; and Hill, ready, watchful, found time to admire the old Mexican's acting. "Thees leetle dreenk for Juanito!"

The jailer exploded in a drunken fury. "You damn Mex ——" The gun in his lifting hand dropped from suddenly limp fingers. His knees sagged. Hill hit him again with the steel barrel of the .45 that had appeared from somewhere under his serape.

Pablo stared, wide-eyed, at the senseless man. His gnarled old fingers made their swift devotional cross. "The Good God armed you," he said, reverently.

Hill was not listening. He was dragging the unconscious jailer inside the office. He had won the breach, but there was so much yet to do, and so little time left.

"We've got to work fast," he said to the almost dazed old Mexican. "We've got to get Sam away from here before the wolves pick up our trail."

CHAPTER SEVEN

Pablo stooped and picked up the jailer's revolver. He thrust it inside his waistband, followed Hill into the office, closed the door and threw the bolt. A knife appeared in his hand as he turned and scowled down at the senseless man.

"He must die, no?" His tone was matter-of-fact.

Hill shook his head, reached a pair of handcuffs from the littered desk. "We'll leave *that* job to somebody else, Pablo." He pulled the jailer's arms behind his back, snapped on the handcuffs and dragged him through the opposite door into a dark corridor that was lined on either side with wooden doors, each set with small iron grilles.

The old Mexican followed, a discontented look in his eyes. The gringo jailer was a rattlesnake. *Verdad! El Señor* was making a mistake. It was wise to always kill a rattle-snake.

A voice spoke softly from somewhere in the gloom of the corridor. "I've been bettin' with myself you'd show up, son."

Hill saw a face peering at him from one of the iron grilles *Sam!*" He wasted no time on more words, bent over the jailer's limp body, straightened up, a bunch of keys in his hand. "We've got to get away from here in one big hurry, Sam." He found the right key for the padlock, swung the cell door open.

"I'm leaving just as quick as you can get this leg-iron off me," Sam Hally said. He was a tall, gaunt-framed man, perhaps in his early sixties, tough as seasoned mesquite from long years of clean living in the open. There was frost in his drooping moustache, and his still keen eyes hinted at the wisdom and tolerance that experience alone can give. He had helped Captain Carnady bring up his first herd of longhorns from the Brazos, and for a score of years after he was HC's trusted foreman. He had put Hill on his first pony, taught him most that he knew of range lore. The affection between them was strong and abiding. He had finally quit his job, and with old Captain Carnady's blessing, had gone into the cow business on

104

his own, forming a congenial partnership with Seth McGee, also a former HC top-hand.

Hill's hands were not quite steady as he removed the rusty manacles. He felt a bit sick. Sam sensed the rage in him.

"Take it easy, son," the old cowman said. "We'll fool 'em yet, you and me and Seth."

"*Señores* ——" Pablo's voice, husky with anger, came from the corridor. "This snake must die ——"

"Put your knife away, Pablo," Sam told the Mexican. "We are not murderers."

He helped Hill drag the still senseless jailer into the cell. "We'll give him a dose of his own medicine, though," he added with a grim chuckle as Hill reached for the rusty chains.

Hill clamped on the leg-iron and fashioned a gag, using the man's own soiled bandana. Out in the corridor again he closed and padlocked the cell door.

Pablo said anxiously, "*Señores* — we must not leave Juanito to hang."

"You can bet your last *peso* we're not leaving Juanito to hang!" The emphasis in the old cowman's voice drew a surprised look from Hill.

They hurried down the dim corridor, peering into the cells. Only one contained a prisoner, huddled in a corner, face grey with terror. It was apparent that Juanito thought a lynching party had come for him. Pablo rapped on the iron grill.

"Juanito," he called softly. "It is your uncle ———"

His wrinkled visage was little more than a blur in that near darkness, but his familiar voice brought the young Mexican to his feet. Hill used his key on the lock, swung the cell door open and in a moment Pablo had his nephew in his embrace.

Sam Hally gave the youth a reassuring smile. "God rides with us, *amigo*," he said. The two exchanged enigmatic looks that again had Hill wondering.

He led the way back to the dingy office. Sam Hally said, "My gun ———" He pawed at the littered desk, frowned, shook his head. "Don't seem to be here ———" He broke off, stared hard at the long-barrelled Colt in Pablo's waistband. "How come you're wearing my gun?" he asked the Mexican. "Sure is my gun you've got there. Cap Carnady had that silver plate put on the butt when he gave it to me — had it marked with my Bar 2 brand."

"Your jailer friend was using it when we grabbed him," explained Hill.

"The low-down thief." Sam beamingly

holstered his recovered gun. Hill slipped the bolt of the outer door, and after a cautious look, stepped into the sunlight. Sam and the two Mexicans followed.

"Which way from here?" Sam wanted to know.

"Over the hill and down to the creek," Hill told him. He studied the dust haze drifting out of Coldwater's main street. Horsemen — a lot of them, and their arrival so early in the afternoon could mean only one thing. A gathering of the wolf-pack. "Let's make it fast," he said.

He led the way through the cottonwoods at a pace that kept his companions almost on the run, halting on the ridge for a moment to gaze back at the ancient adobe building that some two hundred years earlier had been a fort. Those Mexican settlers of long ago had built well, with an eye to defence from marauding Comanches and the massive mud walls had stoutly withstood the onslaughts of time and weather. The gringos had turned it into a common jail, and now it held only one prisoner, the jailer. Hill fervently hoped that the day would come soon when it would be filled to overflowing with the border ruffians who seemed to be turning Coldwater into a rustler's roost.

Big Sam Hally forged alongside as they plunged down the long slope to the cottonwood-fringed creek.

"I reckon you've got horses staked out some place, huh, son?"

"Four of Don Julio's best," Hill told him.

"It looks like you figgered Juanito would be riding with us," Sam commented.

"Juanito was one reason why old Pablo was willing to help break you out of that jail."

"Juanito's only a kid, but he's got the heart of a fighting man," Sam's tone was deeply admiring. "Do you know how come he got locked up in that jail?"

"The jailer said he pulled a knife on somebody and they were going to hang him." Hill shook his head. "I'm thinking there's more to it than that." He gave Sam a brief, inquiring look. "I'm thinking too that you and Juanito have an iron in the fire. You tell *me* why they threw him in jail."

"He was trying to get a message to me," Sam said. "They figgered to stop him."

"A message?" exclaimed Hill. His heart quickened. *A message . . . his grandfather.* He waited for Sam to continue.

"He got a look at me when they dragged him past my cell," Sam went on. "Awful dark in there, but I had my face shoved close to the bars, and so he knew I was there — still alive."

"What makes you think Juanito was trying to get a message to you?" Hill could hardly control his mounting impatience.

"There wasn't a chance for us to do any talking ——" Sam chuckled. "Take it from me, Hill — that kid is smart. He couldn't get to me, so he kept singin' a little song. I savvy Spanish and it sure told me where Seth is hid out. Listen, son ——"

Hill listened, roughly translated while Sam hummed Juanito's little song. *"Señorita, señorita — do not try to flee. Though deep and black the canyon, you cannot hide from me."*

"Plain as the nose on your face," Sam said, when Hill finished. "Black Canyon."

"Black Canyon," agreed Hill. He pushed ahead, not wanting Sam to look at him, sense his disappointment. *Not a message from his grandfather. Nothing to let him dare hope that his grandfather was still alive.*

Sam Hally hastened his stride, overtook him. He had not been fooled — was aware of Hill's torturing thoughts.

"We ain't giving up hope — yet," he said in his calm, deep voice. "Not while you and me and Seth McGee can ride stirrup to stirrup."

"I'm riding in the dark, right now," Hill told him. "We've got to have a powwow, Sam, just as soon as we get away from here. I don't know what it's all about."

They were down the slope now, and pushing through the willow brakes. A voice hailed them softly, in Spanish. They hurried around a dense growth of alders and came to a little clearing. The four horses promised by Don Julio were there, guarded by a lone Mexican rider who showed white teeth in a relieved smile.

"It is good to see you," he greeted in his own tongue.

"It is good to be here, and find these horses waiting," returned Hill. "You need wait no longer, Benito. Make haste and carry the word to Don Julio that Señor Hally and Juanito Sanchez are free men again."

"Si, Señor ——"

"Also assure Señorita Dunbar of our safety." Hill hesitated. "Tell the señorita that I hope to soon have news of her brother."

"Si, Señor ——" Benito's hand lifted in a parting gesture. He wheeled his horse, disappeared in the willow brakes.

Sam Hally was making a careful inspection of the horses. A big grey, suitable for a man of his size, a speedy-looking red bay that Hill immediately preempted, and two smaller, tough-looking buckskins for Pablo and Juanito. A rifle was in each saddle-boot, and a canteen of water and a packet of sandwiches for each man. Don Julio had forgotten nothing.

They wasted no time, mounted and crossed the creek where Hill tossed the jailer's bunch of keys into the deepest pool he saw. Pablo and Juanito exchanged approving grins.

"They wanted to know why I wished to see Señor Hally," Juanito confided to his uncle. "The gringos would have killed me on the spot, only they hoped to make me tell what I knew."

Sam, riding ahead of the Mexicans, overheard. He looked back at Juanito. "You're a good *muchacho,*" he said. And he added with emphasis, "A brave man, Juanito."

The young Mexican spurred alongside. "You got my message, Señor?"

"I sure did, Juanito." Sam's smile was warm with admiration. "Black Canyon, huh?"

"Si, Señor."

"The old cabin," Sam guessed. "You know the place, Hill. You've camped there plenty times — hunting bear."

They came to a small ravine that the day

111

before had been a rushing torrent of storm waters. Only a trickle remained and they followed the wet, boulder-strewn wash until low, bleak hills engulfed them. The trail twisted and looped and finally dropped them into the mouth of a deep gorge from which ran a swift, muddy stream.

Hill gestured for a halt. "Too deep for us to ford."

"That storm sure gouged the old channel," commented Sam.

"Cloudburst up in the high mountains." Hill gave the old cowman a wry grin. "Somebody must have known about that letter you wrote me, Sam. A couple of men were all set to ambush me up on the Borrega rimrock. Raining mighty hard, next thing to a cloudburst and things got mixed up. They shot each other to death." He shrugged. "A lucky break for me — that storm coming when it did."

Sam's eyes lost their kindly expression, took on a bleak look. "Jake Kurtz has been postmaster a lot of years," he said. "Jake's honest and wouldn't tell post office business to nobody."

"He has a couple of clerks," reminded Hill. "Or *did* have the last time I was in his store — a year ago."

"One of 'em is a new feller, since your

time," admitted Sam. He stared with frowning eyes at the swift-flowing, turgid waters of the *Rio San Jacinto.* "I warned you they'd be watching the trails, so it could be just chance that you ran into them fellers."

Hill nodded, swung his horse down hill. There were a lot of questions he wanted to ask, but now was no time. It was important to be a long way from Coldwater before the escape was discovered.

About a mile down the slope they came to a shallows that allowed them to cross, and again they headed up the gorge between high, drawn-in cliffs that shut out the sunlight. The trail was narrow, badly washed in places by the storm, and they were forced to ride single file, with Hill in the lead. Conversation was impossible for the moment, eager as he was to learn all that Sam could tell him. So far, he only knew that Seth McGee was still alive, apparently hiding out up in the forbidding wilds of Black Canyon. He was still completely in the dark as to the mystery that enveloped the ranch. For all he knew, his grandfather was dead, and he feared that any news he might have for Ellen Dunbar about her brother would not be good news.

The dark gorge widened into a canyon with the *San Jacinto* a silver ribbon far below. The trail widened, levelled across a bit of meadow. There were oak trees, and some pines. Hill selected the biggest oak for shade and slid from his saddle.

"Good place to eat our sandwiches," he suggested.

"And do some talking," Sam Hally said.

Pablo and Juanito, with the innate courtesy of their race, moved on to another tree before dismounting. They instinctively knew that the two gringos had much to say to each other.

Hill's gaze followed them. He said, worriedly, "Those two Mexicans have put their necks in a noose on our account, Sam."

"They sure have," agreed the old cowman, his face grave.

"I've been doing some thinking about them," Hill went on. "They've got to ride for the border, stay in Mexico until we make Coldwater a decent place for decent people again."

Sam nodded. His eyes were very kind as he looked at the younger man. "You're real Carnady breed, son," he said. "You see things the way Cap Carnady always did."

"There's a trail heading down to the desert, where the canyon forks," Hill continued. "I'm telling them to take that trail and make dust for the border." He paused, took a bite of his sandwich. "Now give me the news, Sam, and then I'll tell all that's happened since I ran into those killers up on the rimrock last evening." He gave his friend an inquiring look. "Don Julio said they'd thrown you in jail for attempted murder, and there was talk of lynching you tonight. I had to work fast, Sam, pull a surprise."

"I said you think things out like old Cap Carnady," Sam rumbled. He gave Hill a grim smile. "I sure was mighty glad to see you." He chewed thoughtfully on his sandwich. "Ain't much I know, only that hell's bust loose out at HC, and in Coldwater, too, seems like. Seth and me got to wondering why we never see Cap in town, or at the ranch when we would drop in for a 'hello'. Got to wondering too, how come we never see Mat Webster no more, nor none of the old outfit. New foreman there, all new fellers in the outfit. Seth and me didn't take to 'em at all. Border scum, we figgered, the kind of renegades your grandpa could never abide on his payroll."

"Mat Webster gone — all the boys — gone?" Hill eyed the remains of his sandwich with sudden distaste, threw it over a shoulder. "Where are they — now, Sam?"

"All we could learn from the feller who's foreman now, is that Mat lit out for the

115

Panhandle. Went on the prod when I asked him about the rest of the old outfit, said he wasn't paid to keep track of no 'count cowhands."

"And Grandfather?"

The tightness in Hill's voice made Sam wince. He said, slowly, gently, "We've got to hope for the best, son."

"I've got to know — *now*" Hill told him with a savage gesture. "Is — is he — *dead*?"

"I wouldn't know, for sure," Sam said honestly. "All I know is that when Seth and me asked to see him we was told he was too sick for us to see him. We tried it three times and was always given the same story."

"Looks bad," Hill gazed miserably at the older man. "Haven't you talked to Doc Spicer? Grandfather always had Doc Spicer when anybody was sick at the ranch."

"Sure I've talked to Doc Spicer," Sam frowned. "The trouble is he ain't allowed to set foot inside the house. They use another doc — name of Larny — new in town, and he just rings the same bell at me — says it's his order for your grandpa to see nobody without his say-so."

"It's strange you don't see any of the old outfit in Coldwater," wondered Hill.

"Never see hide nor hair of one of 'em." Sam reached for his canteen. He drank, set the canteen down, drew the back of his hand over wet moustache. "Coldwater ain't the town it was a year ago. New man, name of Vince Clayson, runs the OK livery barn. I've a notion old Bill West was scared into selling out to him. Old Bill sure left town in a hurry. Ace Roan still runs the 4-Ace Saloon, but he always was a tricky hombre. New fellow runs the Palace Hotel, name of Curly Teel, an ugly-faced gent I wouldn't trust as far as I could throw a bull by the tail." Sam took another pull at his canteen. "Jake Kurtz and Don Julio are about the only old-timers left," he finished with a sorrowful shake of his head.

"How about Kansas?" Hill asked. "Kansas has lived about all his life on the ranch. Don't you ever see him?"

Sam considered the question, finally shook his head. "I reckon Kansas has gone, too. Heard some talk he was seen in town, but I reckon it was only talk."

"I liked Kansas," Hill said. "He was fast with a gun. We could use him, Sam — when it comes to the showdown." He paused, added softly, "There's Oswen Dern ——" He fingered tobacco sack and papers from the shirt pocket, an odd glint in his eyes as he waited for Sam's answer.

The old cowman glowered. "I was coming

to Dern, and after what he done to me, it's my notion he's back of all this hell we're in."

"I always thought he was a crook" Hill said, thinking of the lawyer's curious handling of Ellen Dunbar's homestead papers.

"Dern's the big man in the saddle right now, for all he's been in Coldwater less than two years." Gloom sat heavily on Sam's craggy face. "Squeezing the life-blood out of the San Jacinto country."

Hill put a match to his cigarette, waited for him to continue. He had never seen the old cowman so seething with rage.

"The thing started when Seth figgered to make another try at getting to your grandpa," Sam went on. "That was three-four days ago, and I ain't seen him nor heard from him since ——" He paused, grim amusement in his eyes — "Excepting what I got from Juanito's little song a while back. Well, son, I figgered Seth had sure run into hot lead out there at the ranch. Anyway, I hunted up the town marshal — a new feller, and found him over at Dern's office, told him I wanted to get up a posse and find out for sure what was goin' on out at HC. This no-good marshal, name of Hancy, told me I was a nosy old mossyhorn, and to get out of town." Sam's fingers curled into

118

a hard fist. "I'm mebbe a mossyhorn, but my horns are still plenty sharp. I smacked him good, knocked him cold, and doggone if that Dern feller didn't pull a gun on me. That's how come I landed in the *carcel,* charged with attempted murder." He wagged his head soberly. "Things sure looked mighty bad, Hill, me in jail, not knowing if you got my letter."

Hill gave him a brief account of the encounter on the rimrock — the meeting with Ellen Dunbar, her rescue from the raiders.

Sam listened intently, his face a grim mask. "Nice kids, them Dunbars," he commented. "Your grandpa liked 'em a lot. He wasn't minding at all for them to homestead the Springs. He figgered the San Jacinto country needed their kind of folks." He shook his head worriedly. "It don't look good for the Dunbar girl's brother."

"She's been through hell," Hill said. He was silent for a long moment, his expression thoughtful. "Juanito," he called. "Come here."

"He's Teresa's grand-nephew," Sam told Hill. "I reckon you savvy Pablo is Teresa's brother. The kid ain't been out of Mexico long."

"Any news of Teresa?" Hill asked, concern

119

in his voice. "Pablo couldn't tell me anything."

Sam shook his head. "Mebbe Juanito can
tell us something." He was studying a cloud
mass pushing above a distant mountain
peak. "Looks like another storm, unless the
wind turns them clouds back," he added
uneasily. "Ain't carin' for a big rain right
now."

Hill nodded, thought of that hour on the
rimrock. Thunder and lightning and rain.
Not just a storm breathing life into the
range, but a dark storm of violence *and
death.* He felt very low, wondered dismally
what the next twenty-four hours would
bring.

Juanito showed signs of near-panic as he
approached. His liquid brown eyes had the
look of a timid deer. Old Pablo stood
hesitantly behind him.

Hill smiled reassuringly, offered his tobacco and cigarette papers. "Have a smoke,
Juanito — you too, Pablo."

"Gracias!" The young Mexican relaxed,
slim fingers busy shaping a cigarette, eyes
questioning the gringos.

"How do you know Señor McGee is up in
Black Canyon?" Hill asked him. "Have you
seen him?"

"No, *Señor.*" Juanito shook his head, went

120

on to explain that a couple of days before the big rain he had been hunting coyotes in an arroyo that in flood time emptied into the *Rio Sombrio* from which Black Canyon took its name. A gringo accosted him, asked if he knew Sam Hally of Bar 2 Ranch. Juanito had replied that he did. The gringo gave him a five dollar gold piece and told him to get to town as fast as he could, ask for Señor Hally at the hotel and tell him his partner wanted him at the old place in Black Canyon. The gringo had made him swear to tell nobody but Señor Hally.

"I could not find Señor Hally at the hotel." Juanito gestured unhappily. "A man there told me that Señor Hally was in the *carcel* and that there was talk of a lynching. The marshal heard me asking for Señor Hally and arrested me when I would not answer his question." Juanito gestured again. "He told a lie, said I had tried to stab him."

"This gringo who gave you the message," interrupted Sam with ill-concealed excitement, "What did he look like?"

"He was tall, and very lean, and had a big nose and a scar on his cheek."

"Mat Webster!" exclaimed Sam. He sprang to his feet. "It was Mat who give him that message from Seth."

"Was that *all* the message?" Hill asked the young Mexican. "No other names mentioned? Nothing said about what he was doing up in Black Canyon?"

"No, *Señor.* I have told you all I know."

Sam was in a welter of excitement. "Let's ride, Hill! Only thing we can do right now is head for Black Canyon where Seth's waiting. And good old Mat Webster. Only one man faster with a gun, and that's Seth." Sam was hurriedly tying his canteen to his saddle. "We'll lick those skunks that's messin' up HC, Hill — get their mangy hides!"

The two Mexicans were watching Hill intently. Intuition told them he was the leader. He got to his feet, snubbed his cigarette under foot. He looked at them thoughtfully.

"It's going to be bad for you two if you're caught," he said. "No need for you to ride with us any more. You've done all you can to help, and now I want you both to head for the border," He gestured. "You know where the trail forks a mile or two up the canyon, Pablo."

Pablo's seamed face set in hard lines, he shook his grizzled head. "Where you ride, we ride, *Señor.* Also I am Teresa's brother — and she is in trouble."

Hill looked at them helplessly, also with deep affection. He felt unable to cope with such fine loyalty. Pie shook his head. "No," he said, his voice not quite steady. "It's Mexico, for you two good friends."

"We ride with you, *amigo,*" insisted Pablo. He gave Juanito a bright look. "Is it not so, Juanito?"

"*Si*" Juanito said. "We ride with our *Señor.*"

Sam, tightening saddle-leathers, chuckled. "I reckon that's *one* problem settled for keeps, son." He stepped into his saddle, swung the big grey away from them. "Let's be hitting the trail."

Hill's voice halted him. "I've got other plans for myself, Sam."

"You ain't coming?" Sam gave him an amazed look.

"Pablo and Juanito are," Hill told him. "I'm heading for the ranch. It's the only way I can find out about things there — about my grandfather."

"We ride with you to the rancho, *Señor,*" announced Pablo. "Juanito and I follow where you go."

"No," Hill said firmly. "Three make a crowd. I will be safer alone."

"You won't last a minute out there," worried Sam Hally.

"You said the hands are all new, and that means I won't be recognized," Hill pointed out. He glanced down at his vaquero garb. "I'll be just another Mexican, looking for a job." He grinned at their dismay. For some reason his decision sent a wave of hope through him, an eagerness to pit his wits against the unknown evil *thing* at HC. "Anyway, I'm riding for Hell Pass and the ranch, and I'm riding *alone.*" He turned to his horse.

Chapter Eight

Ellen came awake reluctantly. The soft bed felt good, and for the moment she was content just to lie there — try not to think. She dreaded the thoughts that would seep into her mind like molten lava.

It was no use. Thoughts came willy nilly, a terrifying resurgence — *her missing brother — red flames in the night — slain horses — violent and dreadful men.* She prayed for strength. It was a time for courage and fortitude — and faith. Hill Carnady had told her never to give up hope.

The thought of Hill Carnady cheered her. He had miraculously appeared from a malevolent darkness in her moment of desperate need. He loomed in her imagination — a fighting angel with spurs and flaming guns. She had never known a man like Hill Carnady.

Thinking of him drew her upright from the pillow. The sun was hardly over the eastern horizon when the elderly Mexican woman had conducted her to this bedroom. She must have slept for hours and hours. She could tell by the direct fall of the thin lance of sunlight through the one partly-open shutter that it must be past noon. Her exhaustion had been so complete she had fallen asleep almost immediately after the woman had put her to bed.

She gazed around, wondering what to do about washing herself. No sign of a basin — or water. The room was fairly large, the *vegas* across the ceiling painted blue. Here and there gay Navajo blankets made colour against whitewashed adobe walls; a large Navajo rug held the centre of the hard, mud-packed floor. A smaller fleecy rug that looked like lamb's wool, was spread close to the massive, four-poster bed.

She had had a skimpy wash of sorts from a small basin before getting into bed. But now she longed for a real bath — hot sudsy water.

Ellen sighed, looked down at the silken blue nightgown supplied by the beaming Mexican woman. It was obvious that Don Julio's retinue included women considerably younger than the elderly housekeeper, and equally obvious that the owner of the nightgown did her shopping in Santa Fé.

She knew from experience that Jake Kurtz did not carry such dainty feminine wear in his store.

She threw back the bedclothes, impatient now to get dressed, bath or no bath. Anxiety was mounting in her. She wanted to see Hill Carnady, learn his plans. It was her premonition that he would want her to stay secure behind Don Julio's high adobe walls, under the watchful eyes of Atilano and Justo. He was due to be disappointed. She had no intention of leaving the brunt of battle to him. This thing was her fight, too. She simply *had* to get news of Dick.

Oswen Dern! Excitement ran through her. She would manage to see Oswen Dern. She did not particularly like the lawyer, but he was shrewd, and would want to help her. It would be less than useless to appeal to Jake Kurtz. The old German storekeeper was kindly and honest, and that was all. She could not hope for help from Jake. And good old Billy West who used to run the OK livery barn was no longer in town. She did not like the new owner of the livery stable, Vince Clayson. He had a sly look to him, and a way of ogling that made her skin creep.

She swung her legs from the bed. The lamb's wool rug felt soft to her bare feet.

She started to slip out of the nightgown, heard a gentle knock on the door — a soft Spanish voice.

Ellen sat down on the bed again. The door opened, revealed a smiling young Mexican girl. A gay-coloured dress and a red and black *mantilla* lay over an arm, and a pair of red, high-heeled slippers dangled from her fingers. Her other hand held a little silver tray with a small jug and a cup and saucer.

"Buenas tardes, Señorita." She came into the room, set the tray down on the small bedside stand. "I am Delfina," she said. "You like nize 'ot chocolate, no?" Her English was pleasantly accented.

"I would like a hot bath even more," Ellen frankly told her.

"Si, Señorita. It come." Delfina glanced over her shoulder, spoke to somebody invisible beyond the door. A stout, grey-haired woman appeared, in one hand a small wooden tub, in the other, a pail of steaming water, and towels over an arm.

"Oh!" exclaimed Ellen. She sprang from the bed. "It looks wonderful! I can hardly wait." Her radiant smile thanked them.

"You 'ave nize long sleep," Delfina told her. "And now you dreenk 'ot chocolate and 'ave nize 'ot bath. Make you feel *muy bien.*" She laid the dress and the red slippers on a chair. "*El Señor* theenk you like keep cool in f-fresh dr-ress." She darted a look at Ellen's travel-stained shirt and jeans, turned to pick them up. "I 'ave them wash for you, *Señorita.*"

"No — please ——" Ellen was already sure that when she dressed again it would be in her own clothes. She went on hurriedly, conscious of surprise and hurt on the Mexican girl's mobile face. "You can leave the dress, though. It was kind of Don Julio to think of it."

Delfina was smiling again. She was extraordinarily good-looking. Ellen wondered if she might be kin to Don Julio — a granddaughter, possibly. If so, she was kin to Hill Carnady — a distant cousin.

"The dress is one of mine," Delfina said. "We are the same size. It would look so nize on you, *Señorita.*"

"This pretty nightgown is one of yours, too, then," smiled Ellen. She was longing to fling it off, use the tub that the old Mexican woman had filled with the steaming hot water.

"*Si, Señorita.*" Delfina looked pleased. "I buy it in Mexico City wheech ees my 'ome. I am 'ere to veesit my Gr-rand-Oncle Julio." Her dark eyes studied Ellen with lively interest. It was plain that she was intrigued by

129

the girl who had so mysteriously appeared at the break of day. *"No habla Español, Señorita?"* she asked.

"Muy poco." Ellen reached for the cup of chocolate. "Very little yet." She smiled over the cup. Her guess about the kinship to Hill was right. It gave her a warming feeling for the pretty Mexican. "I must learn Spanish, because New Mexico is now my home."

"I 'elp you speak *Español* queek. *Más tarde, Señorita.* It mean I see you later, no?" The door closed behind her.

Ellen drained the rich, creamy chocolate, slipped off the nightgown and made for the tub. She was in a frenzy of haste to find Hill before he got away. He might even now be gone. She wished she had asked Delfina — also asked her the time.

She stepped from the tub, dried herself with a big towel, her eyes feasting on the dress Delfina had laid on the chair. It was a pretty dress, a white skirt embroidered with gay little red and yellow flowers. The silk bodice was cut low, and daintily trimmed with exquisite hand-made lace. And there was a silken undergarment, a *camisa,* she guessed, and tucked in one of the red slippers was a silver Navajo bracelet. It was obvious that Delfina had supplied her with the best from her wardrobe. Her affection for this distant cousin of Hill's increased as she looked at the delectable bits of feminine attire. She was enormously tempted to succumb to their appeal. The dress would become her, and it would be amusing to get Hill Carnady's reaction. She was entirely feminine in wanting to please his male eyes. It was possible that he would think her beautiful in the clothes so generously provided by Delfina.

Ellen shook her head. It was no time to surrender to feminine vanity. She must not forget her as yet vague plan to see Oswen Dern. Reluctantly she tore her wrapt gaze from the ravishing dress, turned to her own travel-stained clothes. A thought held her hand. *Whitey — the repulsive albino.* Whitey had followed their trail to Coldwater. He would be on the watch for her. A *malo hombre,* old Pablo Sanchez had called him. She could think of worse names.

Ellen's look went again to Delfina's dress. Whitey would be looking for a girl wearing a blue flannel shirt and jeans — a white Stetson. Delfina's gay little dress would be her passport down the street to Oswen Dern's office. Whitey would not recognize her from the brief glimpse he had had of her in the light of the burning barn. And once she had reached Oswen Dern's office she would be safe. She would ask the lawyer to escort her back to Don Julio's *casa*.

Her decision made, she slipped on the silk *camisa* over her own things, pulled on Delfina's silk stockings and the red slippers with their high heels, She went to the dressing-table and picked up the silver-backed brush and comb the elderly housekeeper had supplied that early dawn. She worked swiftly before the silver-framed mirror, arranged her dark hair in a madonna parting and low on the nape of her smooth young neck. She surveyed the result contentedly. Exactly the way Delfina wore hers.

Gently, she eased into the dress, smoothed the full skirt. It might have been made for her. Delfina was right in saying they were the same size. The tight, low-cut bodice rather startled her, as she gazed at her reflection in the mirror. She had never worn anything quite so revealing.

Ellen shrugged a smooth bare shoulder. For the moment she was a young Mexican señorita.

She flung the red and black *mantilla* over her shoulder. Just the thing to conceal her face when she ventured into the street. Even Whitey's pale eyes would fail to recognize her.

She hid her flannel shirt and jeans, boots

and Stetson, in an empty drawer, took another reassuring look in the mirror and stepped though her bedroom door into a small patio where doves fluttered and cooed around a pool fed by a little fountain. She saw Atilano and Justo, the Yaqui twins, guns in belts, rifles in hands. White teeth gleamed in swarthy faces under tall steeple hats.

"Buenas tardes, Señorita." Their voices sounded like one.

"Buenos tardes," responded Ellen. She was a bit rueful at the immediate recognition. Her gay Spanish attire had not deceived them. After all, she reflected, they had seen her emerge from the room they knew was occupied by the gringo señorita. It would be different, once she was in the street.

She followed a pink and blue flagstoned path that led to another wing. Delfina and old Don Julio stood in a doorway, waiting to greet her. No sign of Hill Carnady, she saw with some surprise.

Misgivings assailed her. It was not going to be easy to leave the *casa* unobserved. High walls everywhere, and massive gates. Her plan to see Oswen Dern was likely to be nipped in the bud. Don Julio would never consent to her leaving the *casa* without Hill's permission.

"Buenas tardes, Señorita" His eyes under

133

their shaggy brows approved her.

"Buenos tardes, Señor." Ellen smiled at him. He seemed like something out of the past, this tall, lean, haughty old man with his fierce moustachios and bristling imperial. A hangover from long gone years when the Territory was still a province of Old Mexico. It was plain that Don Julio Severa was an irreconcilable who had never quite accepted the coming of the gringo. He still clung to the traditions and customs of the *ricos.*

"You 'ave nize sleep, no?" He gestured for her to enter the room. "You now 'ave br-breakfast, no?" He spoke Spanish words to Delfina, bowed — stalked away.

A soft-footed Mexican woman held a chair for her, uncovered a silver dish on the table, revealed a rich-looking stew of meat and vegetables spiced with green peppers and onions and garlic, still simmering and giving out delicious aromas.

"Puchero," smiled Delfina who had taken an opposite chair. *"Sopapillas,"* she added as the woman offered Ellen a plate of little fried cakes.

Ellen bit into one. It was hot and crisp and sweet. She helped herself to the *puchero,* looked inquiringly at the young Mexican girl opposite her.

134

"I 'ave eat," Delfina said with a shake of her glossy head. Concern crept into her voice. She did not like the gringo girl's listlessness, her apparent lack of appetite. "You no 'ongry — no like the *puchero*?"

Ellen put down her fork, looked at her steadily. "I'm wondering about Hill," she said, unaware of her use of his first name. "Where is he?"

"Hillito?" The Mexican girl lifted a shapely bare shoulder. *"Hillito* go away — oh — mooch long before you wake."

"Where has he gone?" Ellen's voice was almost sharp.

Delfina's regretful smile, her vague little gesture, indicated that she had no knowledge of Hill Carnady's whereabouts.

"You eat nize *puchero*," she urged anxiously. "Make you feel *muy bien*."

Ellen picked up her fork. Delfina was right. Food was necessary if she hoped to keep well and strong. She could not afford to starve herself into an illness. To learn that Hill was gone without a word of explanation dismayed her. It was obvious that Delfina was equally in the dark. And it would be futile to ask Don Julio. That haughty old *rico* was not one to answer questions.

Despite her chaotic emotions she found

135

herself eating with increasing relish. The *puchero* was delicious and her naturally healthy appetite made a good sauce. The woman brought her a pot of hot coffee. It was bitter brew, but she found it more to her liking than the too-sweet chocolate. Delfina's soft Spanish voice broke into her thoughts.

"*Hillito* ees co'sin," she said; and went on to explain that their great-grandmothers had been sisters. "W'en thees *malo* war feenish, my pipples go Mexico City."

Very distant cousins, thought Ellen. She looked at the lovely face opposite her, conscious of a twinge of jealousy. *Distant enough for them to marry.* She wondered if Hill might be in love with her. Delfina was attractive enough to catch any man's fancy.

The silent-footed Mexican woman brought in a custard pudding, and some little cakes with raisins in them. Delfina's chatter continued. Ellen guessed that the girl was trying to get her mind off Hill's mysterious absence.

"I go soon to *Americano* school in Santa Fé," Delfina informed her. "I learn spik good *Americano.* I like stay in *Nuevo Mejico* — marry beeg gringo weeth yellow hair." Her low laugh rippled.

"I'll come to the wedding," Ellen promised. *Hill Carnady is Americano,* she thought with another jealous twinge that startled her. *Hill has blue eyes and red in his hair.* She got out of her chair. "The *puchero* was delicious," she told Delfina. "*Muchos gracias,* Delfina." She smiled. "You are a dear and I want you to call me Ellen."

Delfina was out of her chair in a lithe, swift movement that brought her round the shining mahogany table. "Ellen!" she exclaimed, "*querida mia* — you are nize for say that to me!"

They embraced, and Ellen said, looking over the other girl's shoulder at a small door at the far end of the dining-room, "I think I'll lie down again, get some more sleep." *That was surely a key in that door.* She said aloud, almost pleading, "Delfina, I wish you would ask Don Julio about Hill. If he has any news do come and tell me right away. And remembering Delfina's Spanish. "Please, *querida mia!*" *That unguarded door might offer the chance to elude the vigilant eyes of Atilano and Justo.* She forced her attention back to Delfina.

"I weel try, Ellen *querida mia.* If I get thees news of *Hillito* I come queek."

Arms entwined, they sauntered into the little patio. Justo and Atilano, sitting on their heels against the far wall, smoke curling from brown-paper cigarettes, sprang to their feet, teeth gleaming friendly smiles.

"I can't tell them apart," Ellen said.

"Atilano always wear yellow band around his sombrero," Delfina informed her. "Justo's band is red." She added something in swift Spanish.

"I don't understand," Ellen said.

Delfina translated in her halting English, and Ellen gathered that Atilano and Justo were lambs where their affection and loyalty lay, but very fierce tigers against the enemies of their *patron.*

"W'en they swear *por esta cruz,*" Delfina assured her earnestly, "eet mean they die to keep promise." She gave Ellen a hug, turned away. "I weel look for my oncle while you take *siesta,* Ellen *querida.*"

Ellen pretended to be interested in the cooing doves, uncomfortably aware of the Yaqui twins' watchful eyes. They were not forgetting Don Julio's command. A covert look told her that Delfina had vanished inside one of the many doors that fronted on a long *galeria.* She lifted a hand to a shoulder, a little gesture of dismay as if suddenly remembering the *mantilla* purposely left on her chair. She turned swiftly into the dining-room. Atilano and Justo would guess that she had just missed her *mantilla.* Their alert eyes would have noticed its absence from her shoulder.

She snatched it from the chair, hurried to the opposite door, turned the key, found herself in a little alley or lane. The dining-room wing formed part of the wall that surrounded the great *casa*. She was outside, and looking through hoary Cottonwood trees she could see the crumbling ruins of the ancient plaza church.

Ellen wasted no time. She wanted to be in the main street before the Yaquis began to wonder at her non-reappearance from the dining-room. *Mantilla* drawn close to her face, she hurried through the trees. The spindly high heels were not intended for speed, and progress was further slowed by fallen rotted branches and leaves. A twisted ankle would ruin her hopes.

She reached the plaza, paused for a cautious appraisal of her surroundings. Her heart felt like a trip-hammer under the tight bodice. The church loomed near her, a crumbling ruin of adobe and stone. Adobe houses faced three sides of the plaza, most of them badly in need of repair. A few showed signs of life. An aged Mexican, squatting on his heel, back to a crumbling adobe wall, a couple of little children playing nearby, quite naked, but happy. The old man showed no interest in the young señorita passing by. The youngsters paused in their play, gazed at her solemnly. It was her red slippers that drew their eyes, Ellen realized. A woman, evidently their mother, appeared in the doorway, watched with curious eyes until the señorita disappeared around the corner.

In Coldwater's main street at last, Ellen slowed to a sedate walk. Too great haste would attract attention. She passed the dingy Palace Hotel. Horses stood at the long hitch-rail there. A man pushed through the screen door, halted abruptly on the top porch step as he caught sight of her. He wore batwing leather chaps, a tall, arrogant-nosed man with two guns in the holsters that flanked lean hips. He kept his gaze on her until she disappeared inside Lawyer Dern's office lower down the street.

"Strawly," he called softly. "Come here."

Another man pushed through the screen door. He had a shiny bald head, round beefy face and a big paunch.

"Watcha want, Jess?"

"Did you see that Mex señorita go past?" Jess Kinner asked. "She just turned into Dern's office . . ."

The hotel clerk shook his head, fished a cigar from a shirt pocket. "Didn't see her,

Jess. What for you want to know if I seen her."

"I figgered you could mebbe tell me who she is," Jess said. "She kind of hid her face behind her *mantilla* — like she wasn't wanting an hombre to get a good look at her."

Strawly bit at the end of his cigar. "She's likely one of Ace Roan's new dance-hall gals," he guessed. "Ace was talking about a couple new gals." The fat man lit his cigar, grinned. "Drop in at the 4-Ace tonight, Jess. You'll run into the gal there."

"I ain't needing to wait that long," Jess Kinner told him. "I was just heading over to Dern's office when I see her go in."

"He only just got in from the ranch," Strawly said. "He sure looked fit to be tied. What's going on out at HC that's got the boss looking like a bull on the prod, Jess?" The clerk's small mean eyes were like lead pellets in his fat face as he squinted through cigar smoke at HC's tall foreman, "You just come in from the ranch your own self."

Jess Kinner's face darkened. "There's plenty happened." His voice was a curt rasp. "Ain't telling you nothing, Strawly." He started down the porch steps.

The clerk's aggrieved voice followed him. "What for you won't tell me?"

Kinner paused on the last step, glanced

141

back at him. *"En boca cerrada no entran moscas,"* he said with a thin-lipped grin.

"No savvy Spanish," grumbled the clerk.

"A closed mouth catches no flies." The tall foreman winked, crossed the street to the opposite planked walk. Instead of going directly to the lawyer's office, he turned into the narrow alley that separated the building from the 4-Ace Saloon.

Ellen found the front office deserted. Her heart sank. Oswen Dern was not in, despite the open door. She hesitated, wondering if she should abandon her plan for a talk with the lawyer. She dared not be away from the *casa* too long. All she wanted was five minutes with Dern and then she could return, slip into the *casa* through the little door she had left unlocked, gain her bedroom and nobody the wiser. Not even the Yaqui twins.

As she stood there, she became aware of murmuring voices beyond the door of the inner room. Men's voices. A screen door in the back slammed softly, and now she distinctly recognized Oswen Dern's voice greeting the newcomer. The words sounded like *been waiting for you, Jess.*

Ellen decided to make herself heard, attract the lawyer's attention. She returned to the front screen door, gave it a loud slam.

The murmur of voices hushed, and after a moment the door to the inner room opened, framing the lawyer's peering face. He came in, pulled the door shut behind him, looked at her inquiringly. It was apparent that he did not recognize her. It was equally apparent that he was in a bad temper. His eyes were bloodshot, his face flushed, his mouth a thin, hard gash.

Ellen said, timidly, "Don't you know me, Mr. Dern?"

He seemed thunderstruck, gazed at her as if she were an apparition. "Why — my dear Miss Dunbar!" He was suddenly the suave, dapper lawyer again, the anger gone from his face, teeth glimmering under black moustache in a welcoming smile. "No, I didn't recognize you for a moment. What a charming dress. Quite the señorita!" He placed a chair by the desk. "Please do sit down and tell me the reason for this most pleasant surprise."

Ellen took the chair. "I'm in dreadful trouble, Mr. Dern." She tried to keep her voice steady. Putting it into words returned the horror all too vividly. She made it brief. "Raiders burned the homestead to the ground last night — shot my horses — and — and Dick is missing. I'm afraid he's dead." She wiped wet eyes with the edge of her *mantilla.*

Dern's face was a mask of incredulous disbelief and shock. "Miss Dunbar!" Pie stood out of his chair. "I — I am too shocked for words! It — it's unbelievable!"

"It's true, Mr. Dern." She gave him briefly a few outstanding details — the raiders' pretence that Captain Carnady had sent them for her — her brother at the ranch — dying from an accidental gunshot wound — her realization that Captain Carnady could not possibly have sent them.

"He is my friend, Mr. Dern," Ellen asserted. "He wouldn't send men to burn me out."

"Certainly not," agreed the lawyer. He was studying her thoughtfully. "This man you say helped you to escape. Do you know who he is, Miss Dunbar?"

Ellen hesitated. She was reluctant to mention Hill Carnady by name. She knew that his own life was being sought by unknown enemies. She said truthfully enough, "I had never seen him before. He was camping somewhere near and saw the flames."

"He brought you to Coldwater?" Dern's voice was gentle, sympathetic.

Ellen chose to evade the question. "How I got here is so unimportant," she said impatiently. "It's Dick we must worry about, Mr.

144

Dern. I — I'm frightened for him. I'm afraid he's a prisoner somewhere — perhaps dead."

The lawyer nodded, said slowly, "As a matter of fact, Miss Dunbar, your brother *is* out at the Carnady ranch." He paused, added sorrowfully, "It seems to be true that he had an accident with a gun — not serious, I hope."

Ellen sprang from her chair, stared at him, wide-eyed, her face pale. "When did you hear this, Mr. Dern?"

"An HC rider brought the news a few minutes ago," the lawyer explained. He inclined his head at the inner door. "Dr. Larny is waiting in there now for his buggy to be sent up from the OK livery."

"Oh, poor Dick!" Ellen's clasped hands went to her heart. "Oh, Mr. Dern — I *must* go to him!"

"My dear Miss Dunbar — of course you can go to him." He looked at his watch. "We can get you back to your friends again soon after dark. In the meantime perhaps you would like to send them a message?"

"Don Julio's place," Ellen told him. "Yes — yes — he must be told where I am."

"I will see that he is informed," promised the lawyer. He turned to the inner door. "Just a few minutes, Miss Dunbar, while I

145

arrange for the OK to send a buckboard instead of the doctor's buggy." The door closed behind him.

Ellen went to the street door, looked out through the screen. A good many people in town, she noticed. Ranchers and their women, cowboys — a lot of cowboys, for so early in the day. She paced the floor, restless, impatient to be on her way to Dick. Perhaps she was being foolish, but the thought of Dick, dying, perhaps, was more than she could bear. She had no reason to actually doubt Oswen Dern. He was not a type that appealed to her. A trifle too foppish — more like a gambler than a lawyer. But she felt that he was telling the truth, was sincerely wanting to help; and she would be with a doctor. She did not know Dr. Larny — he was new in town, but he *was* a doctor and all the doctors she had ever known were fine, good men.

She found herself gazing at a big Winchester Arms calendar. She had had one like it, given to her by Oswen Dern. *Friday.* Less than twenty-four hours since Hill Carnady had knocked on the door because of her Thanksgiving hymn. It seemed ages ago — an eternity. Not just a few hours, less than eighteen hours since she had ridden with Bat Savan out of the flame-lit yard, her

146

hands tied to the horn of her saddle. How she loathed those men.

The murmur of voices in the other room faded. She heard footsteps, the tread of booted men, the slam of the rear screen door. She began to wonder what was keeping Oswen Dern so long, was tempted to open the inner door and see if the doctor still waited there. The screen door slammed again, more vigorously. She heard footsteps — Oswen Dern. The door opened, and he was there, beckoning to her.

"The buckboard is in the back yard," he told her. "Quickest way to get out of town."

She followed him through the inner room, was vaguely aware of cigar smoke — the smell of whisky. He held the screen door open for her. She ran down the steps and to the waiting buckboard. A man was talking to the driver's companion on the front seat — the tall man with the bat-winged chaps she had noticed watching her from the hotel porch. He turned his head in a curious look at her as she gathered her full skirts and climbed into the rear seat. The stoutish man already sitting there gave her a friendly smile. Dr. Larny, she supposed, recognizing the conventional bag between his feet. She was not attracted by his appearance, his bloodshot eyes, the purple veins on his nose

— the faint aroma of whisky.

They were out of the yard driving up a narrow lane. She could see the sun, midway down the sky, so knew the direction was west.

She closed her eyes, listened to the grind of spinning wheel, the hoofbeats of the fast-trotting horses. She felt suddenly tired, the least bit apprehensive, began to wish she had not been so impulsive. But Dick! She *had* to go to him.

The buckboard lurched round a sharp bend. Ellen opened her eyes. The man sitting by the driver had an arm in a sling, she noticed. There was something oddly familiar about those stooped shoulders. He turned his head and looked at her.

Ellen was unable to scream. She could only stare, dumb with terror. No mistaking those dark, bony features, lips drawn up over long, yellow teeth in a mocking grin — *the brutal face of Bat Savan.*

CHAPTER NINE

Ellen had left the dining-room by the rear
door less than two minutes when the Yaqui
twins saw Delfina reappear from one of the
galeria doors. She halted abruptly, looked
with startled eyes across the walk at the
entrance to the kitchen quarters. Then suddenly she was running, full skirts fluttering
like golden butterfly wings as she disappeared inside the kitchen. She was almost
instantly out again and running towards the
patio.

"Atilano — Justo!" Fright was in her
voice. "Come quickly!" She beckoned them.
"Petra has fainted!"

The Yaqui twins hastily leaned rifles
against the wall and followed her on the run
into the kitchen. Delfina gestured helplessly
at the stout Mexican woman prone on the
smooth mud floor.

"Madre mia!" she exclaimed. "Do something for her. She is too heavy for me to lift."

"The heat," muttered Atilano.

"The heat," echoed Justo.

"Turn her over," Delfina told them. "Throw cold water on her face."

The Yaquis obeyed. Justo filled a tin dipper from a bucket, dashed it in Petra's face. Atilano looked at the girl, worry on his brown face.

"*El Señor* commanded us not to leave the young gringo señorita. We cannot stay here to look after Petra."

"You must get her to her bed," Delfina said. She turned to the door. "I will watch in the patio until you return." She glanced back at the unconscious cook. "Throw some more water on her."

"*Si, Señorita.*" The Yaqui twins scowled at her disappearing back.

"*El Señor* will not like this," Atilano prophesied gloomily.

"He will have our ears if he learns we have disobeyed him," groaned Justo.

Delfina hurried into the patio. The Yaquis had forgotten to mention that the gringo señorita had returned to the dining-room for her forgotten *mantilla*. Delfina had no reason to look inside the dining-room as she passed the door. She was under the impression that Ellen was in her bedroom.

Delfina reached the bedroom door op-

150

posite the fountain. She was about to knock. A thought stayed her hand. Ellen had asked her to question Don Julio about *Hillito*'s whereabouts and bring the news to her immediately. She had found that Don Julio was enjoying his customary *siesta*. She did not dare disturb him. It seemed cruel to disturb Ellen's needed *siesta* just to tell her that she had no news of *Hillito*.

Delfina found a seat by the pool, looked at the cooing doves with eyes that did not see them. She was consumed with curiosity about the girl *Hillito* had so mysteriously placed under Don Julio's protection. She had overheard enough to know that Ellen had had to flee from wicked men who had burned her ranch home. It was all very tragic, and romantic, too, if as she suspected, *Hillito* was in love with the pretty *Americano.* She felt not a shred of doubt about Ellen's feelings for *Hillito.* She was in love with him.

The voices of Atilano and Justo startled her. She had not heard their approach. *Soundless as panthers,* She thought.

"Muchos gracias, Señorita," they said in unison. "We will now resume our guard as *El Señor* commanded."

Delfina rose from the stone bench. "And Petra?" She looked at them inquiringly.

151

"We have carried Petra to her bed," Atilano assured her.

"She called us names for throwing the cold water on her," Justo said.

They picked up their rifles, heads turning in an inquiring look at the bedroom door.

"Be very quiet," cautioned Delfina. "The señorita is now having her *siesta.*"

"Si, Señorita," replied Atilano.

"We will not allow her to be disturbed," promised Justo.

"I will take a look at poor Petra," Delfina told them. "If she is all right, I will myself have a *siesta.*"

"Señorita ——" The twins spoke with one voice.

Delfina halted, looked back at them.

"Please do not tell *El Señor* we left our posts," begged Atilano.

"He would have our ears," Justo said.

"I promise," agreed Delfina. She went on down the pink and blue flagstoned path. "He'd take my ears any day before he'd take theirs," she thought with a rueful smile. *Don Julio just loves those two fierce jungle cats.*

The Yaqui twins sat on their heels, backs to the adobe wall, smoke curling from brown paper cigarettes as they watched contentedly until Delfina vanished inside the hitchen. They took it for granted that

152

she had seen the gringo señorita come from the dining-room with her forgotten *mantilla* and enter her bedroom. Señorita Delfina had assured them that the gringo señorita was taking a *siesta* and must not be disturbed. *Por Dios.* No need to worry about their brief absence from the patio. The little gringo señorita was safe from her enemies while they kept vigilant watch over her.

The mid-afternoon sun found an opening in the great cottonwood trees. Atilano turned his face against its scorching shaft. "My eyes are heavy," he murmured, drowsily.

"I will keep watch while you rest them," Justo said. "Take your *siesta, hermano mio.*"

His fingers worked with brown paper and tobacco. He scraped a match into flame, lit the cigarette. Smoke curled from his nostrils. It was very still in the patio. Only the soft music of the fountain, the coo of doves, the drone of bees in the honeysuckle. Another sound touched Justo's lynx-keen ears — quick-moving feet, stealthy, hushed, as though the runner feared to attract attention. Justo hissed a warning to his drowsing twin and almost instantly they were upright, rifles in their hands.

"Caramba!" muttered Atilano. "It is Benito!"

"*El diablo* chases him," Justo said.

Benito's hands flapped wildly at them as he approached, frantic, beckoning gestures that the Yaquis chose to ignore. They were resolved not to be again lured from their watch on the bedroom door.

"Petra is dying," guessed Atilano.

"It is possible that she is dead," observed Justo.

Benito came to a standstill, glared at them while he struggled for breath to speak. "Donkeys," he gasped. "You stand there like stupid ones while the gringo señorita rides away."

The Yaqui twins looked at him, speechless, disbelieving.

"*El Señor* will have your ears," scolded the breathless vaquero.

"*Loco!*" hissed Atilano. "You have the bad dream!"

"The gringo señorita is now in there — having her *siesta.*" Justo gestured at the bedroom door.

"I have just seen her with my own eyes," Benito told them. "From my post on the watch tower. It is she, in the clothes she wore when Señor Hillito brought her this early dawn." Their incredulity was driving the vaquero into a frenzy. He shook fists at them. "It is the gringo señorita I tell you —

154

wearing the same white hat, the shirt and pants of a man."

Despite their disbelief, Benito's vehemence impressed the Yaquis. They exchanged uneasy looks, both of them recalling the few minutes they had left their post to attend the ailing cook. Their heads turned like puppets on a string in doubtful looks at the bedroom door. They began to run.

"*Señorita!*" Atilano rapped softly on the door.

"*Señorita,*" echoed Justo. "We would hear your voice!"

No voice answered them from beyond the door. Dismay, fear, filled their eyes. Atilano reached for the iron latch. It lifted without resistance. The door swung open to his cautious push. He peered into the room. Justo peered over his shoulder.

"She is gone!" Their voices sounded like one, dismayed, horrified.

"The white hat, the blue shirt — the pants of a man — gone," Justo said unhappily.

"We saw her with our own eyes run back into the dining-room for her *mantilla,*" recalled Atilano. "She was wearing the dress of Señorita Delfina. It is the work of *el diablo.*"

"Or it is possible that Señorita Delfina deceived us," muttered Justo. "It was she

155

who called us to attend Petra whose faint was perhaps a sham."

"Quick!" groaned Atilano. "Let us go to the tower and see with the long glass what Benito has seen."

"*Si,*" agreed Justo. "If it is indeed the gringo señorita — we will overtake her — bring her back before our *Señor* hears this terrible news."

Silent as ghosts they hurried with Benito along the pink and blue path. Undue noise would arouse Don Julio from his *siesta,* bring down an immediate avalanche of wrath on their heads.

They paused for a minute to hasten into the dining-room. It was Justo who found the rear door unlocked. "She deceived us," he groaned.

"We thought she was but going back for her *mantilla,*" Atilano reminded. He turned fierce eyes on Benito. "Quick — find out if she was seen when she fled through the plaza."

Benito nodded, sped into the cottonwood grove. Justo and Atilano ran swiftly, silent as stalking jungle cats. In a few moments they were up on one of the watch towers, raking the landscape beyond the creek with the long telescope.

"I see her!" exclaimed Atilano.

Justo snatched the brass telescope from him. "A grey horse," he muttered. "Not one of ours . . . she is down from the saddle — unfastens a pack and places it on the ground. He continued to peer intently through the telescope. "It is our gringo señorita, now again wearing the white hat and the shirt and pants of a man." He relinquished the long glass to his twin's impatient hand.

"*Si.*" Atilano shook his head. "It is the work of *el diablo.*" His voice hardened, showed alarm. "A rider watches her from the willow brakes. He stalks her like one who means harm."

He lowered the telescope to its box under the stone walk "Quick! We must ride — pronto."

They were throwing on saddle gear, drawing leathers tight, when Benito made a breathless appearance. "She was seen in the plaza!" Benito gave them a wild look. "It is very strange. Señora Cordero swears the señorita she saw in the plaza was wearing a dress, and *not* a white hat and the shirt and pants of a man. Señora Cordero says she thought it was our own Señorita Delfina who hurried past, her *mantilla* hiding her face."

The Yaqui twins exchanged grim looks.

Justo said, "While we were in the kitchen with Petra, the gringo señorita got her man clothes and fled from the *casa.*"

Atilano nodded. "When you looked through the long glass she took a pack from her saddle. Our Señorita Delfina's dress which she plans to hide in the chaparral."

"The grey horse she rides is from the OK barn," Justo guessed. His eyes were hot with anger. "We must ride fast, *hermano mio,* bring her back before the news reaches Don Julio."

"Si!" Atilano's voice was tight with anxiety. "I do not like the way that rider watches from the willow brakes. She is in great danger." He was up in his saddle, horse leaping under the gouge of spurs as Benito opened the great gate.

Justo, also in his saddle, reined his plunging horse. *"Amigo,"* he warned Benito. "Do not tell Don Julio this bad news. His anger will destroy us." The Yaqui's face hardened. "If the worst happens and he must be told — it is our Señorita Delfina who must face him."

The vaquero lifted both hands, palms out. "I would sooner face a mad bull on foot than carry this news to *El Señor. Si* — I will give your message to our Señorita Delfina."

He stood for a long minute, anxious gaze

following the Yaqui twins. *"Verdad!"* he ejaculated aloud. "The anger of *El Señor* is more terrible than *twenty* mad bulls." He closed the gate, threw the bars, hurried to resume his post on his watch-tower. . . .

Lucy Royale carefully tied her horse to a sapling willow on the edge of the brakes. She was in haste to get at her paint box — and to work. Clouds moved and changed so quickly, and the great cloud mass pushing above the distant peaks against the deep blue of the New Mexican sky fired her with eagerness to get it all on canvas. The dark, towering peaks, the thunderheads, so ominously black at the base, their proud crests taking on the iridescent pink from the mid-afternoon sun.

She unstrapped her case, set up the little easel and frowningly studied her assortment of paints. She would want to get in that deep yellow of the far-flung desert, the touches of green, sagebrush, mesquite — the great, tumbled boulders. The thunderheads must come first, she decided. The colours would be gone if she waited too long, wasted time on the foreground.

Somewhat to her surprise she became aware of an odd nervousness, a growing apprehension — a feeling of insecurity. *It's the vastness of this country,* she tried to assure herself. *Makes one feel so alone and help-less — just a speck of dust. And everything is so still — and those thunderheads do look threatening.* She snatched up palette and brush. *Silly, silly,* she scolded herself. *Get to work.*

She stood there, gazing up at the distant mountain peaks — the thunderheads, and wondering what had got into her. Something had taken her inspiration. She could only stare with blank, unseeing eyes, the brush a useless thing in clenched fingers. *Something has frightened me,* she thought. *Something terrible — malignant. I wish I could hear Dad's voice — Bill's voice.*

She thought of Bill Wallace, her father's assistant. Big, shy Bill. He wanted her to marry him, take her to his Scottish high-lands. She would be Lady Lucy — wife of Sir William Wallace.

Something stirred behind her. Lucy forced herself to turn and look. Her horse, head high, ears pricked forward. Her gaze fol-lowed the direction of those pointing ears.

The man rode slowly towards her from the willow brakes A cowboy, from the looks of him. Lucy's fears began to fade. Cowboys were always courteous to women. No reason to be afraid of this lone rider.

He slid from his saddle, stood by his horse, and now she saw he had a gun in his hand and that his lips were curled back from too-prominent teeth in an oddly triumphant leer. Her fears were back again, sent shivers prickling up and down her spine. She tried to speak, could only gaze at him, the fear plain in her eyes.

"I reckon you're remembering me." His voice was a nasal whine; and still looking at him, Lucy saw that he was an albino and that there was wicked malice in his unwinking pale eyes. She drew on her courage, forced herself to speak.

"I never saw you before in my life," Lucy told him.

"No use lying," Whitey said. "I boosted you into your saddle only last night when Bat took you off while me and Kickapoo finished setting the house on fire."

"I don't know what you are talking about, and I wish you would please go away." Lucy's anger was getting the best of her fears. She thought she had never seen so repulsive a man. She stamped a small, booted foot. "You heard me!" Her voice was sharp, contemptuous. "Please go!"

Whitey's pale eyes took on a cold glitter. "You ain't fooling me none, pretending you're not the Dunbar gal."

"Well, I'm *not*!" snapped Lucy.

He grinned, eyed her from head to foot. He had seen Ellen Dunbar only briefly when putting her on the chestnut mare in the glare of the burning barn. The levis, the blue shirt — the white Stetson hat, were enough to satisfy him.

"Ain't no other gal wears a rig like you got on," he told her. His high nasal voice took on a threatening note. "Some feller shot Bat and got you away from us, but I picked up your trail into Coldwater."

"I'm *not* the Dunbar girl," Lucy said desperately. She was remembering something Jake Kurtz had said about another girl who had been in his store, buying levis and blue flannel shirt and white Stetson hat. It was the clothes that this dreadful creature was really recognizing. They had convinced him that she was the Dunbar girl.

He lifted his gun, motioned her to her grey horse. "You sure took my fancy when I boosted you into your saddle last night. I ain't losing you a second time."

Panic seized Lucy. "I'm *not* the Dunbar girl!" She almost screamed the words.

His hand was suddenly on her arm, his fingers like steel claws. "You're forkin' saddle now if you've got good sense."

Lucy hung back. "Where are you taking me?"

"I ain't takin' you to HC for the big boss," Whitey told her with a grin. "Me and you is heading for the border.'

Lucy hit him with the palette still in her hand. Whitey swore, let loose of her arm to wipe his paint-spattered face. Lucy started to run, blindly, heedless of direction. She heard a shot — a terrified yell from Whitey. She did not even turn her head to look, could only keep on running — stumbling, towards the willow brakes. A horseman was suddenly reining close to her side — a swarthy, fierce face under a tall steeple hat, but the face wore a smile, friendly, appealing.

"Señorita! Señorita! Me Atilano — *amigo!"*

Lucy slackened to a walk, face upturned to him. He patted his chest. "Me Atilano," he repeated. *"Amigo, Señorita mia!"*

Lucy came to a standstill, stared up at the smiling brown face. She knew that *amigo* meant friend. Who he was or where he came from she had no idea. Only that he was a friend — a miracle.

She dared now, to look back. Another swarthy, stocky man was approaching, leading his horse. He carried a long knife and when he halted close to her she saw that the

163

blade was wet and red. He sensed her shock, bent quickly and stabbed the blade into the sand, again and again, gave her a reassuring, apologetic smile and thrust the cleaned knife inside his shirt.

Atilano got down from his saddle, teeth glinting white in his brown face as he gestured at the other man. "Justo," he said, *"Hermano."*

Lucy looked at them. Brothers, of course, and twins. They were like two peas in a pod. The one who said his name was Atilano wore a yellow band around his sombrero. The band on Justo's hat was red. She had the odd feeling that they seemed to know her and took it for granted that she knew them. Atilano's mention of their names was merely to reassure her that she had nothing more to fear. Also it was plain that they understood English even less than she understood Spanish. She called on the little she knew.

"Gracias," she said.

They smiled. *"Por nada."* They spoke with one voice.

Lucy gathered they were politely waving away her thanks — that what they had done was a mere nothing. She ventured a look back at her grey horse. Something lay on the ground a few yards from her easel. She

164

repressed a shudder, averted her gaze from the dead man and went stumblingly to a boulder and sat down. She hoped she was not going to be sick. Death had been very close to her, too.

One of the towering thunderheads spat lightning, thunder rolled and echoed from the high peaks. A storm was in the making. *Lightning, thunder — rain,* she thought. *I've just been through a storm more dreadful than anything Nature can do.* She managed to find her voice. "I must go home," she said to her pair of guardian angels." She gestured at her horse — at her easel. She could not summon the fortitude to go near that dead thing lying near them.

They understood her gesture, if not her words.

"*Si.*" Atilano nodded, glanced at the dark cloud mass funnelling over the mountains. "Rain," he said. He made a wide gesture. "Beeg." He followed Justo to the grey horse. Lucy did not look again in that direction. She could hear them talking, and though their Spanish was meaningless to her, she sensed that something deeply puzzled them.

"The dress of our Señorita Delfina is not in this box," Atilano said. "It is very strange, *hermano mio.*"

"Where did she get this box with its paints

165

and brushes?" Justo wanted to know.

Atilano folded the easel, packed it in the case and closed the lid. *"Quien sabe,"* he grumbled. "Let us not worry about what we do not understand."

"Verdad." Justo nodded. "We will be glad that we found her in time to save her from the gringo snake."

Atilano picked up the splintered palette. "She broke it over his face, filled his eyes with paint. He would have killed her but my bullet got him first."

"I finished him, sent him to *el diablo,"* Justo said complacently. He patted the knife inside his shirt, glanced at the dead man. "We will leave him to the buzzards, no?"

"Si." Atilano picked up the paint kit and went to the grey horse. "We must ride fast — get back to the *casa* with the señorita before Don Julio discovers her absence."

Justo went to Whitey's horse, standing with reins dangling on the ground. He fastened the reins loosely to the saddle horn, gave the horse a hard slap. The horse lunged forward, disappeared in the chaparral. Satisfied, the Yaqui hurried to overtake Atilano who was leading the grey on its tie rope.

Lucy heard their approach, gave Atilano a grateful little smile when she saw that he had fastened her paint kit to the saddle. She mounted, picked up the reins.

"Gracias," she said.

The two Yaquis sprang up to their saddles. Justo shifted his horse to the girl's other side so that she was placed between them with Atilano still holding the grey on the tie-rope.

Lucy held out a hand for the rope. "I will go back to Coldwater now. Give me the rope."

"We ride with you, back to the *casa,*" Atilano said gently, but firmly. He held on to the tie-rope.

Lucy did not understand the words, but there was no mistaking his intention to hold her horse on a lead-rope. She repeated the one word that made sense.

"Casa?" Her bewilderment was plain. "I do not understand. Please give me the rope."

The Yaquis exchanged puzzled looks. They had seen Ellen Dunbar only briefly when Hill Carnady had brought her to the *casa* that early dawn. She was then wearing the blue shirt, the white Stetson — the pants of a man. When they had their second and third glimpses of her she was wearing their Señorita's gay flowered dress. They were not really any too familiar with her face, but

167

they were as sure of her identity as they were sure of Don Julio's wrath if they failed to get her back to the *casa*. The fact that she now wore the clothes she was wearing when she arrived was proof enough. She was the gringo señorita who had so strangely disappeared, wearing the flowered dress, a mystery they were content to leave unsolved.

Justo said, sorrowfully, "She pretends not to know us."

Atilano touched his head significantly. "It is the shock the gringo snake gave her. That explains why she does not know us — her good friends."

Lucy looked at them with growing uneasiness. She wished she could talk to them in their own language, make them understand. Atilano's little gesture had not escaped her. They thought she was out of her mind.

Lightning flared over the mountains, thunder reverberated from crag to crag. Nature's storm was fast overtaking them. *I'm not finished with my own dreadful storm.* she reflected unhappily. *Oh, what shall I do?*

The Yaquis were again exchanging Spanish words, and she saw real anxiety on their brown faces, gentle appeal in the looks they gave her.

"*Si,*" Justo said. "Her mind is sick. We must care for her gently, keep her from harm as we swore to Don Julio."

Atilano nodded, gave Lucy a warm, gentle smile that told her more than words. "We *amigos*," he said. He crossed thumb over forefinger. *"Por esta cruz,"* he said, earnestly.

"Por esta cruz!" echoed Justo, his own thumb crossed over forefinger. "We *amigos.*"

Lucy offered no more resistance, rode between them, the grey's lead-rope in Atilano's hand. *I'm in God's care,* she told herself. *But oh, such strange angels!*

CHAPTER TEN

Dr. Homer Royale scrambled from the ledge and gave his assistant a curiously awed look. "If I know my business, Bill, and I think I do, this butte is loaded with copper." The geologist dusted his hands, reached for his pipe. "Biggest find since the old Santa Rita."

"Good news for Oswen Dern," commented young Wallace. He gazed up thoughtfully at the giant butte. "Not that I'm shouting with joy for him," he added with a wry grin. "I'm nae likin' that Dern chap much, Chief. Usin' the talk of the Territory, I'd say he's one sure mean hombre."

Dr. Royale put a match to his pipe. "Something snaky about the man," he admitted. "His morals are not our concern, though." His look went to the blackened ruins of the Dunbar homestead buildings. "Dern will have a shock when he hears of the fire that has wiped out his new camp."

"Struck by lightning, Piute claims," Bill Wallace said. "Yesterday's storm." He shook his head doubtfully. "I'm thinkin' there's something queer about that fire, Chief."

"Queer!" Dr. Royale gave his assistant a sharp look. "What do you mean, Bill?"

"Those horses," Wallace said, "lying there in the ruins of the barn. They were badly charred, but not enough to prove the fire killed them."

"What do you mean?" repeated Royale.

"I took a look at them," Bill told him stolidly. "Bullets and not fire, killed those horses."

"You're a suspicious Scot," grumbled the geologist. "It's possible that they were shot to end their sufferings. It's difficult to rescue horses from a burning stable." He shook out his pipe, returned it to a pocket, glanced apprehensively at the black thunderhead overhead. "Looks like another storm coming up fast. Let's get started back for Coldwater. Nothing more to do here."

Lightning forked from the massed clouds, thunder rolled and big drops of rain splashed on their startled faces. The two men began to run stumblingly down the boulder-strewn slope, Bill Wallace carrying the canvas bag that held the geologist's outfit. They could see the buckboard, with

Piute in the driver's seat, waiting on the road outside the fence that enclosed the charred remains of the burned homestead. A lone horseman appeared from the chaparral, reined to a standstill some hundred yards from the buckboard. Lightning forked again from the sullen cloud mass and a titantic crash of thunder appalled the ears of the running men, brought them to a staggering halt. Rain came down in a roaring deluge that momentarily blotted out the landscape. A shout reached them faintly through the deafening inferno, and of a sudden the curtaining, drumming rain passed on and they saw their buckboard, overturned and dragging at the heels of the stampeded team. The lone rider was already in the road, in chase of the runaways. In a moment he was alongside, hand reaching for a bridle.

"He's got them stopped!" Dr. Royale wiped his steaming eyes. He gave the younger man a grim look. "That lightning hit too close for comfort, Bill."

Bill's keener gaze was fixed on something lying in the road not far from the fence gate. "Too close for Piute, I think, Chief," he said.

Dr. Royale muttered a startled exclamation, stumbled on down the rain-slopped hill. Bill Wallace passed him, was the first to reach the limp body lying in the road. "He's dead, Chief," he said, when Dr. Royale reached the scene.

Royale could only nod sorrowfully. Excitement, his hurried descent, had taken his breath. Bill's look went thoughtfully to the charred embers beyond the fence. "It *could* have been lightning that set fire to those buildings," he said, "After all, it was lightning that got Piute. I'm thinking you are right, Chief, about the horses over there in the ashes. They were shot to save them from burning to death."

The geologist found his voice. "Of course," he said, gruffly. "Teach you a lesson, you suspicious young Scotsman." He glanced at the distant mountains, veiled by rain. Lightning stabbed the dark sky there, thunder rattled and drummed. From the hillsides came the sound of rushing little streams, and from the river below them, the muted roar of flood waters.

"Here comes that chap with our buckboard team," Bill Wallace said. He added in a surprised voice, "He's the Mexican who passed the hotel this morning — the one who refused to let Lucy sketch him."

Dr. Royale was not caring who the man was. He beamed at the tall Mexican on the red bay horse. "You have our thanks, sir,"

173

he greeted courteously. "That was fast work, saving our team for us."

"Ees no'ting, *Señor,*" returned Hill Carnady, careful to keep recognition and curiosity from his eyes. He motioned for Bill Wallace to take the team trailing on his rope. He longed to ask what business had brought these men to Red Butte Springs, decided to let them do the talking.

"You did not bring the buckboard," Dr. Royale continued. "I suppose it is broken?"

"*Si, Señor.* Mooch broke — all beeg smash." Hill's look went to the dead Piute.

"Our driver," Dr. Royale told him. "That bolt of lightning killed him."

Hill concealed his recognition of the dead man. Piute had once been a member of the HC outfit, a no-good scamp his grandfather had warned out of the San Jacinto country on pain of dangling at the end of a rope for brand-blotting. It was plain that the renegade had returned from south of the border to join the mysterious gang now threatening the ranch and the life of its aged owner. He could feel no regret for Piute's demise. He managed a sorrowful shake of the head for the benefit of the two strangers, listened in silence while they exchanged worried words.

"A damnable situation," the grizzled-bearded one was telling his younger companion. "Piute dead, our buckboard wrecked, and here we are miles from the hotel."

Bill began stripping the harness from the horses. "We'll ride 'em home bare-back," he suggested.

Dr. Royale looked at the horses with dubious eyes. "I'll be a wreck, too, by the time we get back to Coldwater," he objected glumly. "I haven't ridden bare-back since I was a youngster."

Bill's look fastened on Hill Carnady's saddle. His face lighted. "How about a deal with our Mexican friend?" he again suggested. "You can make it easy with a saddle under you." He grinned. "I won't mind losing a little skin, riding *my* horse bare-back."

Dr. Royale turned an interested look at the saddle under the red bay's statuesque rider. He wished that he could speak Spanish, or that the Mexican could speak English. He placed a hand on the saddle, drew his purse from a pocket. "Me buy," he said, and shook gold pieces into his palm. "Me give plenty money for saddle."

No hint of the amusement he felt showed on Hill's poker face. He shook his head, hand lifting in a gesture of refusal so definite that Dr. Royale reluctantly returned the gold pieces to his purse.

Bill Wallace's face darkened. "Listen!" he exclaimed "this gentleman is Dr. Homer Royale, one of the world's most famous mining experts, and he's an old man. Have a heart, fellow!"

"Old man your eye!" remonstrated his boss indignantly. "Damn it all, I'll ride the brute bare-back if that's what you think of me!"

Hill's gesture for their attention interrupted the argument. "*Señores* — I 'ave those saddle." He was recalling the saddles of Topaz and Pedro he had left in the cave on Piñon Mesa.

Relief was in the looks they bent on him, and Dr. Royale said feelingly, "Young man, you're literally saving my hide. But by what magic can you produce a pair of saddles from your sleeve?"

Hill was studying him with odd intentness, and there was a glint in his eyes quite misunderstood by the others. They thought that the apparently simple Mexican was fired by the problem of saddles. He was thinking of the name he had just heard. *Homer Royale. A name he had heard mentioned with reverence many times during his more than a year at the Colorado School of Mines. The noted geologist and mining expert.*

176

Homer Royale — whose books on mines and mining were the last word. He understood, now, what had brought this grizzled-bearded man of the mining world to the San Jacinto country — to Red Butte Springs. He was not alone in suspecting the possibility of vast wealth locked away in HC's bleak hills and buttes. It explained the sinister web that had entangled his grandfather and he believed that he could name the man responsible. As yet he had no proof — must go slow — smell out the trail that would lead him to the arch-conspirator who planned to possess the Carnady ranch. He heard the younger man's voice, rough with suspicion.

"Acts verra queer, if you want my opinion, Doctor. A wild look in his eye, the same as I've seen when one of my gillies ran smack into a stag he'd no idea was there. Completely confounded the man was, I remember."

"Now, Bill ——" Dr. Royale's voice was gentle, placating, as if sensing some tremendous mental turbulence troubling the tall man on the red bay horse. "Give our Mexican friend a chance to pull a couple of saddles from under his hat."

"Reminds me of old Sandy MacGregor," muttered the young Scotsman. "Always seeing spooks ——"

177

Hill paid no attention. Eyes narrowed under the dripping brim of his hat, he was deliberately studying them, trying to come to a decision as to their honesty — their unawareness of anything wrong. He could not bring himself to believe that the great Dr. Homer Royale would knowingly be a party to the evil that seemingly stemmed from the little cowtown of Coldwater. And the tall young Scotsman was too obvious for a second thought. As if wanting to give him time to miraculously produce the promised saddles, Dr. Royale's voice rambled on.

"Strange that lightning should strike a second time so close to this place," he said to his companion. "Yesterday, this camp of Dern's, and today, our poor driver."

Hill stiffened in his saddle, ears alert as the two men talked.

"If it hadn't been for what happened to Piute just now, I'd have sworn those buildings had been set on fire by human hands," Bill Wallace declared. "Piute told us it was lightning, but those horses made him out a liar at the time. All four of them shot in the head."

Dr. Royale was weary, disgruntled — worried about the trip back to Coldwater. "Why bring *that* up again?" he said testily. "Of course it was lightning set the place afire."

"Piute seemed verra anxious to keep me away from those burned horses," Bill Wallace said, a stubborn look hardening his bony face. "He was nae likin' for me to look at 'em, Chief, and that's what got me to thinkin' that it was nae lightning that set the place afire."

Hill Carnady spoke softly from his saddle. "*Si, El Señor* say w'at ees tr-true. *Malo hombres* burn leetle *casa* ——" He gestured at the gutted barn — "burn all — keel 'orses ——"

They stared at him in shocked silence; and the complete consternation he read in their eyes brought him to his decision. These men were unaware of anything wrong, had not the least idea of what was going on. He was tempted to shed his Mexican vaquero role — tell them the truth. He resisted the impulse. Too much was at stake. A mistake could mean disaster — death. The life of his grandfather — the Carnady ranch, everything he held dear, was at stake, depended on what he did or did not do. He thought of Ellen Dunbar, and his resolve hardened. For the time it must be a lone fight. To divulge his identity to Dr. Homer Royale could be the fatal blunder. Dr. Homer Royale was a great mining expert, but even great men could be bought if the reward was big enough. He heard the geologist's voice, harsh, suspicious, now:

"Stop talking nonsense and get those saddles you say you have somewhere near."

"*El Señor* no theenk I say tr-rue thees place 'ave been burn by those *malo hombres?*" Hill's hand lifted in a hopeless gesture. "I say tr-rue wor-rds, *Señor.*" He gestured again, swung the bay. "You come, *Señores* — I take you to those saddle."

They followed him, Bill Wallace leading the buckboard team. A few yards up the slope, Dr. Royale halted, gazed back at their dead driver. "We shouldn't leave him lying there in the road," he worried.

"Best place to leave him," Bill Wallace said. "The sheriff, the coroner — or whoever looks after these things in Coldwater, will want to see just what happened." He gave his boss a mirthless grin. "We nae want anybody to think we murdered the man."

"That's right," agreed Royale. "After all we *are* strangers here."

Overhead the sky was a deep blue, but far to the west, lightning continued to flare from the clouds that blanketed the high peaks; thunder rolled, touched their ears like the muted beats of great drums; and all about them was the sound of rushing little streams on their downward plunge to the Rio San Jacinto.

Hill, his ears alert, heard the voices of the two men trailing his horse.

"Damn queer, what this Mexican claims really happened to Dern's new camp," Dr. Royale was saying. "I'll have to ask Oswen Dern about it. He certainly spoke of a new cattle camp he'd recently built at Red Butte Springs. You heard him, Bill."

"My hearing is verra good," the young Scot said dryly. "I heard what Mr. Dern told you when he asked you to have a look at the butte. I remember he said that if there was gold or silver in that red butte he'd be using the place for a mining camp and not a cow camp."

"There is gold there, and silver," Dr. Royale said. "Those specimens he showed us were good enough to make me want to have a look at the place." Excitement deepened the geologist's voice. "Dern can forget about what little gold and silver he'll ever mine from that butte. The man will likely drop dead with joy when I tell him that his red hill is loaded with copper. Millions and millions. The biggest find since the old Santa Rita."

"A lucky man," commented Bill Wallace. "For all his good luck I have nae likin' for

181

him. I'd nae trust him with a penny of mine."

"You're a dour suspicious Scotsman," grumbled his chief. "I should send you back to your stags and gillies."

"I'm only waitin' for Lucy to say the word, sir — and you'll be wanting a new assistant."

Dr. Royale gave the tall young Scot a kindly look. "You have my blessing, lad," he said.

They were up on Piñon Mesa now, and no more talk came from the two men. Only the crunch of boots on wet earth, the flinty strike of shod hoofs on loose stones. They reached the cave where Hill had cached the saddles of Topaz and Pedro. He swung from his horse, turned and looked intently at Dr. Royale, a searching, probing look that put a puzzled frown on the bearded geologist's face.

"I breeng saddles," Hill said. "*El Señores* plees no come." He pulled at the brush that concealed the opening to the caves, and vanished into the darkness beyond.

"What's eating him?" Dr. Royale pulled nervously at his grizzled beard. "I've never seen such bleak rage in a man's eyes."

"I'll tell you what, Chief ——" Bill Wallace hesitated. "These Mexicans are proud chaps

182

— and he wasn't likin' you callin' his story about that fire down there *nonsense.*" Bill nodded. "You as good as told him he was a liar."

"He doesn't understand English well enough to know what the word *nonsense* means," Dr. Royale protested.

"It's the way you *said* it," Bill maintained.

Dr. Royale stroked his beard thoughtfully. Perhaps he should have given the young Mexican a chance to explain his curious assertion that *malo hombres* had burned the Dern cattle camp. He had allowed his excitement about the rich copper lode to interfere with good manners. And Piute's tragic death — the loss of the buckboard, had shocked him tremendously. He had been so keen to get back to Coldwater — report his amazing discovery to Oswen Dern.

Hill appeared from the black mouth of the cave, a saddle and blankets under either arm. Dr. Royale studied the supposed Mexican curiously while the two younger men threw the saddles on the horses, adjusted bridles and tightened cinches.

"I wonder where he got that red in his hair," he said in an aside to Bill Wallace as the Scot adjusted stirrups to suit his long legs. His beard twitched in a grin. "Looks like some red headed Scot has been making love to the señoritas in this neck of the woods."

"Don't forget the Irish," chuckled Bill Wallace. "Not that I'm saying any good Scotchman would pass up a pretty señorita if she tossed him a smile."

"Be careful," muttered Royale. "The man may understand English better than he can speak it." He gave Hill a keen look, detected nothing in the poker face to indicate that their personal remarks had been understood. Again he produced his purse, shook out gold pieces, frowned at Hill's quick gesture of refusal to accept pay for his services.

"These saddles," protested Dr. Royale. He touched them. "We must pay you for these saddles — at least ——"

"*Gracias — no, Señor* ——" Hill's smile was thin, his voice chill. "Those saddle geeft to Señor Dern. Señor Dern like 'ave those saddle."

The bewildered geologist slowly pocketed his purse. "The man has me puzzled," he said to Bill Wallace. "His manner tells me that he shares your dislike for Oswen Dern. Perhaps there's some truth in his story about the fire down there." He waved in the direction of the burned homestead.

Hill nodded, hot anger suddenly in his eyes. "*Si, Señor — malo hombres* 'ave burn those place — keel those 'orse — try steal leetle gringo señorita."

Dr. Royale slowly climbed into his saddle, lifted the reins, hesitated, turned a troubled look on the puzzling Mexican with the red in his hair.

"What is your name?" he asked curtly.

"Rubio, *Señor ——*"

"That's for his red hair," the geologist said to his assistant. "I wish to heaven I could speak Spanish," he added irritably. "If Dern is not the owner I'd like to know it."

"Leetle señorita 'omestead those place." Hill gestured down at the great butte. "Leetle gringo señorita own those place — not Señor Dern."

The great mining expert sighed, shook his head. "The man has me wondering," he said to Bill. The worry deepened in his eyes. "I'm not liking this business, Bill."

"Begins to smell," Bill said.

"There are millions at stake," fumed Dr. Royale. "If this Mexican is telling the truth, that copper-loaded butte belongs to some unknown girl who has been run off her homestead. I've heard of such dastardly things," he added, musingly. "And come to think of it, there is little law in this remote

185

corner of the Territory. Anything can happen."

"Only the law of claw and fang," commented Bill Wallace. "The law of gun and knife — the strong against the weak." The young Scot's bony face was suddenly a grim mask. "I'm repeatin', Chief — this business smells — to put it mildly."

His boss nodded, his own bearded face grim, determined. "I'm asking Oswen Dern to explain," he said. "He's got to have a good answer, or I'll expose him."

"His answer could be a bullet in the back, a knife in your ribs," warned Bill Wallace. "Take it easy, Chief. There's Lucy to think of — and Coldwater has the looks of a tough place, to me."

Dr. Royale gazed at him, something like fear in his eyes. It was plain that the thought of his daughter jolted him.

"You're right, Bill," he muttered. "We must use caution. . . . Can't risk harm coming to Lucy. Wish to heaven I'd sent her and her paint box off to Europe instead of bringing her out here to this lawless border country." He lifted his reins, smiled at the tall, silent Mexican, called upon his little Spanish. *"Gracias, Rubio, amigo.* You *bueno hombre."*

"Hasta la vista," Hill said courteously, his

own smile warming the hard set of his face. *"Vaya con Dios, Señores."*

He watched them ride down the hill, restraining eagerness to be in his own saddle and on the trail for Hell Pass. He did not want them to notice in which direction he rode. He could still make the ranch by nightfall. The darkness would suit him — give him time to do some scouting. Once at the ranch house he would need to use his wits. One wrong move could mean a fatal bullet — and the end for his grandfather — if the old cattleman was still alive. He hoped that he would be able to get in touch with old Teresa. For all he knew she might be dead. Not even Sam Hally had been able to give him news of loyal Teresa Sanchez. If his old nurse should be alive and if he could get to her, her help would be invaluable. Teresa could tell him much that would fill out some of the blank pages.

Hill made a cigarette, his gaze on the two horsemen making their slow way down the boulder-strewn hillside. His brief encounter with them had been a bright light in the darkness through which he had been floundering. He was reasonably certain now who was responsible for the terror that was throttling Coldwater — the Carnady ranch — the burning of the Dunbar homestead. Dr.

187

Homer Royale had said enough to explain his presence in the San Jacinto country. Oswen Dern was the man who had employed the noted mining expert. The scheming lawyer had become aware of the possibilities of vast mineral wealth locked away in the hills and buttes on the Carnady range and was making certain that no obstacles would keep him from realizing his ambition to control any valuable deposit the geologist might find. Not even murder was going to stop the man. For some reason he had decided that the Red Butte Springs homestead was too valuable to let remain in the hands of the Dunbars and he had resorted to the ruthless means of the country to wipe out these unwanted homesteaders.

Hill got up from the sun-warmed boulder, shook out and retied his slicker to the saddle. He took a worried look at the mountains. Thunderheads still hung low there, and he thought of Sam Hally up in Black Canyon, searching for Seth McGee's hideout. Sam would find things tough up there, unless the storm made a quick sweep into the west. He recalled Sam's words about Oswen Dern. *The big man in the saddle right now. . . . Squeezing the life-blood out of the San Jacinto . . . I've a notion he's back of this hell we're in. . . .*

Hill clenched a fist until the knuckles showed white. He longed to return to Coldwater, get Oswen Dern under his gun. An insane thought, he told himself. When he returned to Coldwater it must be with force strong enough to control the lawless element there. He would need good fighting men, like the old HC outfit and its hardbitten foreman, Mat Webster. It was an odd story Juanito had told about Mat Webster. The tall, lean gringo with a scar on his cheek, who had accosted Juanito in the Black Canyon country could have been none other than the missing Mat Webster.

The thought that Mat was still alive and apparently in touch with Seth McGee sent a thrill through him. It was possible that others of HC's staunch outfit were not far away, were awaiting the call that would muster them to battle, a call their old boss was unable to send.

Hill dropped his cigarette, stamped the smouldering tip into wet earth under boot heel. *Ride for Hell Pass on the jump, son. We're needing you. . . .* That was what old Sam Hally had written in that urgent note. It was the call to arms that the old HC outfit was waiting for — a call from old Captain Carnady's grandson.

Hill lifted his face to the clean, rain-washed blue sky. He could still dare to hope — carry on the fight. He could not — must not, let his friends down, men like Sam Hally, Seth McGee — good old Mat Webster and his fighting riders. He thought of Ellen Dunbar. She, too, had put her faith in him, was depending on him — on his courage — his wit. He was glad to remember that she was safe behind Don Julio's high, guarded walls.

His gaze went down the slope. Dr. Royale and his companion were disappearing around the great butte, well on their way back to Coldwater.

Hill rolled another cigarette, watched until they vanished, his eyes hard, thoughtful. He had given the great mining expert something to think about, perhaps done enough to upset Oswen Dern's dreams of empire. The thought of what Dern would think when he saw the saddles sent to him as a "geeft" from an unknown Mexican gave him a certain grim pleasure. There would be men in Coldwater who would recognize those saddles as the property of a pair of killers known as Topaz and Pedro. Dern would correctly guess that his plan to ambush Captain Carnady's grandson had met with failure — realize that his hired assassins were lying somewhere in the chaparral —

190

food for the buzzards. He would want to know just how Dr. Royale had come into possession of those saddles. He had a feeling that the geologist would use discretion — refrain from a too life-like description of the unknown Mexican who had come to his aid. Dr. Royale might decide that it was best not to mention the red in the Mexican's hair. Dern would jump to the correct answer. He would know that Captain Carnady's grandson was still alive — and on the warpath, and the knowledge would put fear into his heart, leave him squirming — wondering from which direction his nemesis would strike.

Another thought came to Hill, one that worried him. Dr Royale's assistant had frankly hinted that Dern might decide to make certain Dr. Royale did not live long enough to expose him. Dern was the power in Coldwater — his hired killers would not hesitate to put an end to the geologist and those with him, including the girl. It was a troubling thought that sent an ugly tingle down Hill's spine. He could only hope that the young Scotsman would be on the alert. The dour Highlander had impressed him as a fighting man who would not be easily caught unawares.

Hill snubbed his cigarette under boot heel,

got into his saddle. As Teresa would say, *It was in the hands of the good God.* He turned down hill for the river road — for Hell Pass.

CHAPTER ELEVEN

Jake Kurtz stood in the doorway of his General Merchandise Store, worried speculation in the eyes behind his steel-rimmed spectacles as he watched the men grouped in front of Roan's 4-Ace Saloon across the street. There was something ominous about them, in their low-voiced talk, their furtive glances up and down Coldwater's drab little main street. Other men were gathered on the hotel perch and down by Vince Clayson's OK livery barn. There was a look of expectancy about them, as if they awaited a signal that would send them hurrying into their saddles.

"It does not look goot," muttered the old German store keeper. "Somet'ing iss bad going to happen."

A lanky, middle-aged rancher pushed out from the dark interior of the store, a horse collar hooked over an arm. Kurtz gave him a troubled look. "You go qvick, mein friendt

— get your vife away qvick."

The rancher's look went up and down the street. The low sun struck little glints of silver from pools left by the thundershowers. He nodded, said grimly, "I've been hearing some talk, Jake ——" He shook his head. "But what can *we* do to stop it?"

"Only the goot Gott can stop it," Jake said solemnly.

"This cowtown has gone to hell," the rancher said in a voice hardly above a whisper. He glanced apprehensively at the little group across the street. "Poor old Sam Hally — as fine a man ever lived."

"You go qvick," reiterated Jake. He flapped a hand at the sunbonnetted woman on the seat of the light ranch wagon waiting at the hitch-rail. "Get your vife away qvick."

"I wish to God I could do something," half groaned the rancher. His sunburned face was pale.

Jake Kurtz could only look at him, shake his head, gesture again at the ranch wagon.

The rancher took a step, paused. "Thanks for keeping my credit good, Jake," he said awkwardly. "I reckon next year's crop will put me on my feet."

The old storekeeper gave him a kind look. "Let me the vorry do about your bill, mein friendt," he admonished gently.

194

The rancher hitched the new horse collar over his arm, said simply but feelingly, "If this San Jacinto country ever amounts to anything it will be because of men like you, Jake." He stamped down the porch steps, climbed into his wagon and sent his team into a brisk trot.

Jake turned into his store, spoke curtly to his young Mexican assistant. "Lock the door, put up the shutters, Felipe. Ve close now — qvick."

"Si, Señor ——"

Jake looked at the Mexican thoughtfully. "You keep avay from street, Felipe," he said gravely. "You tell your people all avay keep — stay inside."

"Si, Señor," Felipe nodded, fear in his eyes. It was plain that he too, had heard talk.

There was plenty of talk going on in Oswen Dern's office. He sat behind his desk, glowering at his four companions with hard, angry eyes. A close observer might have detected in the lawyer's manner, a certain apprehension — a desperately concealed fear.

"All right," he said to HC's new foreman, "Just how *did* Seth McGee get loose — take young Dunbar away with him?"

"No sense you going on the prod, boss," Jess Kinner sulkily protested. "All I know is

195

they busted out of the granery where we put 'em. Kickapoo was laying inside, knocked cold, tied hand and foot and his two guns gone along with his holster filled with .45 shells."

Vince Clayson, owner of the OK livery barn, showed tobacco-stained teeth in a mirthless grin. "Your first blunder, Jess," he said, "was not making buzzard's meat out of Seth McGee the moment you laid your gun on him. That jasper's a dozen wild cats wrapped inside one hide and he sure can think faster than the devil."

The arrogant-nosed HC foreman gave him an ugly look. "Too bad you wasn't there," he said resentfully.

"Vince has an idea, at that," Ace Roan broke in. "Jess should have handed McGee a dose of lead when he had the chance, and that's what I'm thinking about Sam Hally. We've got him locked up in the jail. Why waste time waiting for dark? Let your boys get to work — get him to dangling on a rope." The saloon man nodded, chewed on his unlit cigar. He was a heavy-shouldered man with purple veins in a red face and tobacco stains on his greying, drooping moustache. "Let's get to work on Sam Hally right now," he rumbled.

"I'm voting with Ace," declared the fourth

member of the group facing the little lawyer behind the desk. He was a long, thin man, with parchment-like skin drawn tight over a bony face and slits of eyes sunk deep under hairless sockets. "What's the sense — waiting for dark? Turn the boys loose now on Sam and that Mex kid."

Oswen Dern looked at him. Curly Teel was perhaps the least dependable of this hired quartette of border renegades. He was supposed to be the legal owner of Coldwater's Palace Hotel, which he was not, any more than Vince Clayson was the owner of the OK livery barn, or Ace Roan the proprietor of the prosperous 4-Ace Saloon. The deeds to the several properties were in Dern's name and in his strong box, and these men were important citizens only as long as they were of use to him. They knew that he held the power of life and death over them. A word to certain sheriffs ——

He sent a sly look at Jess Kinner, scowling his resentment at the criticisms his friends had been sending his way. He held the same power over the truculent HC foreman, with the difference that Jess knew too much about him, in fact enough to return him to prison for the rest of his life — even to the gallows. It was at this moment that Oswen Dern made one of his ruthless decisions.

An accident must very soon happen to Jess Kinner — a *fatal* accident.

His hand lifted in a gesture that silenced them, froze their attention. "Stop your fool bickering." His voice was the hard, sharp edge of a razor. "I'm not blaming Jess for what happened out at the ranch." His eyes stabbed at them. "And don't forget who is the boss here ——"

"You don't need to look at *me,*" blurted Ace Roan. His red face took on a mottled look. "I wasn't figgerin to buck you — or Jess, when I spoke like I just done."

Dern's cold look rested on him for a brief moment, swung to Curly Teel, who lifted a hand in a panicky gesture.

"I'm riding with Ace on that, boss," mumbled the hotel man over his chewed cigar.

Vince Clayson's grin met Dern's questioning lift of eyebrows. "Quit the beefin', boss," he rumbled. "Give us the bad news." His grin shifted to the other men. "I reckon you've heard the one about fellers that don't hang together gits hung anyways."

"Shut up," Dern told him angrily. "Watch your tongue, Vince, or you won't live to be hung."

The long silence was broken by Ace Roan. "I'm needing a drink," he croaked with a wry grimace at Vince Clayson. "Hangin' talk gets my throat awful dry." He tossed his chewed cigar into the brass spittoon.

"Me, too," muttered Curly with a sour look at the liveryman. "At that I should be getting back to the hotel. Promised Strawly I'd take the desk for him a couple of hours."

Dern hesitated, with obvious ill-grace produced a flask from a drawer. Vince Clayson reached a long arm across the desk for it.

"*Gracias,* boss ——" He took a drink, passed the flask to Curly Teel.

"You know about the Dunbar girl," Dern said. His teeth showed in a fleeting, cruel smile. "She got away from Bat Savan last night, but she's on the road to the ranch to join old Carnady. She's another ace card we're holding."

"Sure was queer, the way she come walking into your office," chortled Curly Teel. He passed the flask over to Ace Roan. "A innercent little fly walking so nice into the spider's parlour." The hotel man reached for the flask again. "I'm betting you was some surprised, boss."

"I'd like to know who it was got her away from Bat and brought her to Coldwater," worried Dern. "She admitted she was staying with old Julio Severa."

"We gotta get rid of that old Mex hombre," growled Ace Roan.

"He keeps more than a score of armed men behind those high walls of his," reminded Oswen Dern. "And don't forget that there are a lot of Mexicans in this town — more than a hundred."

Jess Kinner came out of his sulks, snatched at the flask Curly had returned to the desk. "My boys can handle those hombres," he said. "Say the word and we'll stampede 'em away from here like a bunch of frightened sheep." He took a long swallow, slammed the flask back on the desk.

"We'll attend to old Severa later," Oswen Dern told them. "Right now we have more important things to do — old man Carnady, Sam Hally and Seth McGee."

"Why don't you finish old Cap Carnady off and be done with him?" grumbled Curly Teel. He grinned, reached for the flask again. "We've got Sam Hally all ready for a hang-tree party and we don't need to worry none about that little wildcat pardner of his."

"Won't take no time for the boys to smell out Seth McGee's trail," agreed Jess Kinner.

"It's not so simple as that," Dern said. "We don't want too much excitement in this town while that mining expert, Royale, is here. He'll be finished with his work in a few days, and when he's gone we can attend to old Julio Severa and the Mexicans."

"We can fix him, too," Curly Teel said with his ugly grin. "Close his mouth for keeps if he gets too nosey."

Dern shook his head impatiently. "Royale is too big a man in the mining world," he pointed out. "It is known that he is here in the San Jacinto country. His disappearance would mean dangerous inquiries." He glanced through the window at the fading sunlight. "Royale should be back most any time now with his report on Red Butte Springs," he added.

"I reckon the boss is right," agreed Vince, thirsty gaze on the whisky flask. His hand slid across the desk. "Here's hoping the feller has big news for you, Boss." He tilted the flask to his lips.

"There is something else that worried me a lot more than Severa or Dr. Royale," Dern continued, frowning at the liveryman, "and that is old Carnady's grandson, Hill Carnady." He paused, reached out a hand for the half-empty flask. "No more drinking, boys. You've had enough." He dropped the flask in the desk drawer. "I'm not liking the fact that we've had no word from Topaz and

Pedro." His eyes questioned the liveryman.

Vince shook his head. "They ain't showed up at the barn," he said.

"There is only one answer," fretted the lawyer. "Hill Carnady was too smart for them."

"Meanin' that Topaz and Pedro is laying some place in the chaparral, huh?" growled Curly Teel.

Dern nodded, fingers tapping nervously on his desk. "Somebody got the Dunbar girl away from Bat Savan," he reminded. "We know that Hill Carnady was headed this way. It begins to add up. Hill Carnady is somewhere close and on the loose." Dern shook his head. "I don't like it. Young Carnady is more dangerous to us than all the others combined."

"You should fix that old longhorn grandpa of his pronto," again suggested Curly Teel.

"Not yet," Dern said. "I'm needing Cap Carnady's signature on some papers."

"You can write his name just as good as he can." Jess Kinner's tone was significant. His lips twisted in a sardonic grin at the lawyer.

Dern ignored him. "I've got the old man believing that we have his grandson in jail, here, and that he'll hang alongside Sam Hally if those papers are not signed by noon tomorrow."

"We've got Sam Hally in the *carcel,* all right," Vince Clayson said sourly, "But we sure ain't got young Hill Carnady waiting there for that noose." He muttered a surprised oath. "There goes that mine fellow now, him and his helper." He held the shade aside for his companions to see into the street, turned his head in a stupefied look at Dern. "Piute rode 'em out to Red Butte Springs in the buckboard, and now they're headin' for the stable, ridin' the team and with saddles under 'em, too." The liveryman's voice was a hoarse croak. "I'm crazy in the head," he groaned. "I'm seein' things ____"

"Don't be a fool!" Dern was careful to conceal his own gnawing fears. "Get down to the barn on the jump, Vince. Find out what's happened."

The liveryman nodded, slammed through the door. Dern's look went to Curly Teel. "You, too, Curly. Get back to the hotel. Royale won't take those horses to the barn. He'll offsaddle at the hotel."

The hotel man got out of his chair. "He was looking kind of grim when he rode past," he said. "He looked mighty upset, if you ask me, boss."

"Get over there and find out." Dern's attempt to keep his voice smooth was wearing thin. "And Curly — listen ——"

The hotel man stared back at him sullenly from the partly-opened door, panic only too apparent in his sunken slits of eyes.

Doing some fast thinking, decided the lawyer. *Getting set to make a jump for the border.* "Listen, Curly," he repeated, softly, "Watch your step when you talk with Dr. Royale and don't get fool notions. Savvy?"

Curly nodded. "I reckon I get what's in your mind," he said.

"Get back here as quick as you find out what's happened to Piute and the buckboard," Dern ordered. "And Curly, tell Dr. Royale I'll be obliged if he will step over to my office and let me see his report on Red Butte Springs."

The confidence in his voice, his cool smile, seemed to reassure the hotel man. He nodded again. "Sure, Boss. I'll be right back." The screen door closed behind him.

Conscious that Ace Roan and Jess Kinner were watching him with ill-concealed curiosity, Dern fingered a cigar-case from an inside pocket of his tailored linen coat. He was not going to let Ace and Jess suspect the fear that squeezed his heart. He selected a cigar, carefully trimmed the end with the little gold penknife on his watch-chain, put a match to it and leaned back in his desk chair.

"I wasn't liking Curly Teel's manner," he drawled.

Ace Roan nodded. "Acted like the devil was on his tail," he said. "I'd bet he had the border on his mind." Ace chewed on his unlit cigar, spat at the brass spittoon, shrugged a heavy shoulder.

Jess Kinner glowered at the tips of his hand-made leather boots, shook his head at Dern's questioning look. "Curly is *your* business, Boss. Right now I'm setting here for you to say the word about Sam Hally." The HC foreman went to the window, lifted the shade for a look into the darkening street. "Cain't keep my outfit standing' round *too* long, and them dozen other fellers you told me to bring to make it look good."

"Steff Hancy should be back from Hatchita any minute. We've got to wait for Steff to get here, Jess. Steff is Coldwater's town marshal and we want his story that he tried his best to keep the lynchers from taking Sam and that Mex kid away from him."

"You do too much damn planning," growled Kinner. Delay was making him ugly. "Where's that bottle you hid away, Boss? I'm craving a drink."

Ace Roan tossed the remnants of his chewed cigar into the spittoon, pulled another from his shirt pocket. "I'm sure riding with Jess on that," he declared. He rolled drink-inflamed eyes at the tall foreman. "A hang-tree party calls for plenty likker, huh, Jess." His big hand slapped the desk. "Bring out that bottle, Boss — and we'll say a long *adios* to Sam Hally." The saloon man's hand gestured at the door. "Listen to 'em, Boss! The likker is sure hottin' 'em up good for a necktie party."

Dern did not favour him with even a glance. He leisurely opened the desk drawer, set the whisky flask on the desk. "Help yourself, boys." His tone was affable. They would have been surprised had they guessed his longing to reach for the little, but deadly derringer inside his coat pocket. From the street, where the evening shadows were now crawling, deepening, came low, ominous sounds, the distant low growl of an angry, rising surf. Impatience was seizing Jess Kinner's riders — the border renegades he had gathered for the hanging of Sam Hally and the young Mexican. Dern wondered vaguely about the Mexican. He only knew that Steff Hancy had thrown him in jail because he had been heard asking for Sam Hally. The town marshal was taking no chances, not even with a youth like this Juanito Sanchez who would soon be kicking at the end of a rope.

Dern looked thoughtfully at the two men finishing the flask between them. Like Vince Clayson and Curly Teel, these two renegades were as dangerous to him as Curly Teel and Vince Clayson, and for the same reason. Loyalty was not in their blood. They possessed courage, but loyalty was something beyond their understanding.

Dern stared down at his twiddling fingers, unaware of the dreadful grimace that twisted his lips, drew the startled looks of Jess and Ace. His mind was racing down the years. *College, the top man of his class — law school — his growing fame as a trial lawyer — and then forgery — prison.* He was not then known as Oswen Dern. Only Jess Kinner knew his true name. He had saved Jess Kinner's neck in those good days. Only Jess Kinner knew the truth about him — knew his real name. Jess would have to go, join a dozen and more others who had mysteriously disappeared. Curly Teel, too and Vince Clayson and Ace Roan, when they were no longer of use to him. He would make a clean sweep of all the border scum on his payroll. He would be the big man in the San Jacinto country, lord of a vast empire — the richest, most respected citizen in the Territory. He would rebuild the little cow-town of Coldwater — make it the thriving centre of his domain. A woman would be needed to add lustre to his respectability — a wife worthy of the honour. He thought of Ellen Dunbar. She was attractive — knew her way around — *but* she also knew too much about him. Ellen Dunbar would have to go, too — be buried along with the others in the dark past he was determined to put behind him — *forget*.

CHAPTER TWELVE

The hurried tramp of booted feet pounding up the planked walk snatched Dern from his momentary dreaming. Curly Teel pushed through the door. Vince Clayson, close on his heels, broke the news.

"Boss ——" The liveryman's eyes were bulging — his voice hoarse. "The mine feller says they got them saddles from a Mex hombre, and Boss — Topaz and Pedro was riding them saddles when they went to lay for Hill Carnady up on the Borrego rimrock."

Dern showed no hint of the chill gripping his spine. He looked questioningly at Curly. "What did Royale tell *you*?" he asked.

"Same story," answered the hotel man. "Seems like the storm hit 'em hard over at the Springs. Lightning knocked Piute dead and the team beat it away from there on the run. This Mex feller chased 'em, got 'em stopped, but the buckboard was smashed

209

up bad."

"Did Royale say where this Mexican found the saddles?" Dern knew it was a question that he could answer better than Curly.

The hotel man shook his head. "He claims he was too glad to have the saddles to be askin' where the Mex hombre got 'em from."

"I sure know them saddles," Vince declared. "Looks like the Mex feller took 'em from the broncs Topaz and Pedro was riding when they left here for the Borrego rimrock." The liveryman gazed around at his companions, a look of maudlin triumph on his face.

"Meaning that Topaz and Pedro were then dead men," interpreted Dern with a thin, contemptuous smile, "it's my guess you stopped at the 4-Ace for a couple of quick ones, Vince, and that's why your mind is so quick on the trigger." Dern's look went deliberately to each of the four men, "Listen," he told them, his voice almost a snarl. "I'm paying you big money for your trigger fingers, so lay off the whisky. Savvy?"

It was Jess Kinner who answered him. "Sure, Boss. We savvy plenty." His voice and eyes were surly. "Just don't keep us waiting round too long. I crave action."

"You're due for more action than you'll be wanting, Jess," Dern told him. His thin, black moustache lifted in a vicious smile, and his look questioned Vince and Curly. "Did Royale describe the Mexican — mention red in hair?"

The two men shook their heads. "I wasn't asking him what the Mex looked like," Vince said.

"What the hell does it matter what the Mex looked like?" the hotel man wanted to know. "These Mex fellers look all alike to me."

"Not *this* Mexican," retorted Dern. "I'm betting you Dr. Royale could have told you that his Mexican had red in his hair and that means it was Hill Carnady who dug up those saddles, and only God knows what else he gave Royale in the way of information about what's going on."

There was a long silence, touched only by the diapason growl of voices in the street.

Jess Kinner, said, uneasily, "The boys is getting some impatient, Boss ———"

"I'm just trying to tell you that Hill Carnady is here — on the loose with his guns." Despite the effort for control, there was panic in Dern's voice. "He's already left Topaz and Pedro lying some place on the Borrego rimrock — shot Bat Savan and got

211

the Dunbar girl away from him. If she hadn't been a little fool she'd be safe now, where he took her, behind Don Julio's high walls, instead of heading for the ranch with Bat riding herd on her."

"I'm wondering where Whitey is at," Vince said. "He was in town come dawn, stabled his bronc for a feed."

The HC foreman scowled. "He sure ain't in town, now. We could use that fast-shootin' little devil."

Oswen Dern nodded. He knew of only one man faster with a gun than the deadly little albino renegade. Hill Carnady — now already too close — too dangerous to be allowed to live. He came to a decision.

"All right, Jess," he said to the HC foreman. "No sense for us to wait longer for Steff Hancy to get back from Hatchita. You go get your outfit started for the jail — and make it look good. Tell Pinto to put up a fight."

"I'll leave him locked up in one of his own cells." Jess was on his feet, hands caressing gun-butts on either lean hip. "Don't worry, Boss. I'll make it look so good nobody will figger you and the marshal was back of it."

"Fine, Jess ——" The lawyer's smile was warm, friendly. "Drop in when it's finished and we'll open a fresh bottle."

"Sure will, Boss ——" The tall renegade HC man hitched again at gun-laden holsters, unaware of Oswen Dern's significant look at Vince Clayson, a look that meant he would not return from the hanging of Sam Hally. "The whole damn outfit'll be gettin' drunk tonight, Boss," he said complacently.

Vince Clayson got heavily to his feet. "I ain't seen a necktie party for most six months," he said. "I reckon I'll mosey along with you, Jess . . . mebbee help pull on the rope." He dropped Dern a sly wink, significantly patted the gun on his right hip.

Ace Roan and Curly Teel got out of their chairs, both of them announcing their intention to climb the hill for the pleasure of seeing Sam Hally "dance on air".

"You said you had to relieve Strawly at the desk," Dern reminded Curly Teel, moustache lifting in a satirical smile.

"I ain't missing this fun for nobody," declared the hotel man. "Strawly can go jump in a *cholla* if he don't like it."

An ominous sound flooded into the office as Jess Kinner pulled at the door, the tumult of the mob lusting for excitement — action. Torches began to flame in the street, and above the chilling roar of the surging crowd was another sharper sound — the quick, hard rap of bootheels on the planked sidewalk — a man running — a man in desperate haste.

He plunged through the open doorway into the office, halted, struggling for breath, his eyes wild, terrified, fixed on the man behind the desk.

"What's wrong, Steff?" Dern motioned for Jess to close the door, shut out the uproar. "What's wrong?" he repeated. He was already guessing the truth.

"He's gone!" gasped the town marshal. "Hally went and busted out of jail — him and the Mex kid, Juanito Sanchez."

Jess Kinner rapped out an oath. Curly and Ace and Vince could only gape at him, eyes disbelieving. Dern said in a hard, tight voice. "Sit down, Steff. Make sense out of your story."

The town marshal reached for a chair which creaked under his some two hundred pounds. "I just got in from Hatchita," he said. "Went straight over to the jail and found the door locked. Had to get Ike Jones over from his blacksmith shop with a crowbar and pry the door open ——" Town marshal Hancy paused, wiped his perspiring face with the grimy handkerchief he fumbled from a hip pocket.

"All the keys gone from the office," he yelped. "Had to use Ike's crowbar to bust into the cell where Pinto was laying gagged and handcuffed."

"What is Pinto's story?" Dern asked. "There must have been outside help."

"Pinto claims it was a coupla Mex fellers pulled the job," the town marshal told his interested listeners. "One of 'em was old Pablo Sanchez, uncle to that Juanito kid I'd throwed in jail."

"Did Pinto recognize the other Mexican?" Dern's fingers drummed on the desk and his face had a grey look. Steff Hancy's reply came as no news to him. He was already certain of the man's identity.

"Pinto claims he'd never laid eyes on the feller before." The town marshal paused, a curious expression on his beefy, sunburned face. "Pinto's mebbe lying, but I'm thinking he's talking gospel truth ———"

Oswen Dern interrupted him. "I can tell you what Pinto said." The lawyer's smile was acid. "Pinto told you that the Mexican had red hair?"

The town marshal gaped at him. "How come you know the Mex had red hair?"

"It's simple," answered Dern. "Pinto's red-headed Mexican was Hill Carnady." The lawyer frowned at Curly and Vince. "Dr. Royale could have told you that *his* Mexican had red hair, too, if you'd asked

215

him. Hill has Spanish in him. His grand-mother was old Don Julio's sister. He can make up like a Mexican — speaks Spanish like a native."

Curly Teel was not liking Dern's sarcastic smile. "The old mine feller was some grumpy," the hotel man said resentfully. "As good as told me to mind my own business when I asked him about the Mex."

"You gave him my message?" Dern asked.

"Sure did. He said he wasn't figgerin' to see you tonight about that report." Curly sent a dark brown stream at the brass spit-toon. "Seems like him and the young feller are some worried about the Royale gal. She ain't got back yet from her paintin' trip."

"Got caught some place in that storm," surmised the town marshall.

"I told the gal she should have a guide along with her," grumbled Vince Clayson. "Awful easy for a stranger to get lost out in the chaparral."

Jess Kinner muttered an imprecation. "It's Hill Carnady I'm thinking about, and Sam Hally." He fastened impatient eyes on Dern. "What are we waiting for, Boss?"

Dern nodded. "Get your outfit headed back for the ranch," he told the HC fore-man. "Hill and Sam will make for the ranch — try to get old Carnady away from us."

"We're leaving for HC on the jump," declared Kinner.

Dern regarded him thoughtfully. The unexpected crisis was forcing a change in his plans about Jess Kinner. Not until Hill Carnady and Sam Hally were dead men could he afford to lose Jess.

He said, softly, "I'm leaving it to you, Jess. Make sure of the job, this time."

"We'll get 'em," promised Kinner. He pushed through the street door, into the darkness, and they heard his voice bellowing to his riders.

Quick-moving feet came pounding up the planked walk.

Curly Teel gave Dern an apprehensive look. "Here comes the mine feller," he said.

Dr. Royale, with Bill Wallace at his heels, burst into the office. The geologist fastened an angry look on the hotel man.

"Teel!" he exploded. "I thought I told you to round up men and horses and start a search for my girl. Why are you wasting time here?"

"I was just telling Dern and Marshal Hancy about her being lost." Curly gestured. "No sense our riding off everyway."

"That's right, Doctor." Oswen Dern's voice oozed sympathy. "We were just deciding where to look first. This is a big country."

"Let's start," gruffed Lucy's worried father, glowered at the livery man. "Clayson, bring a couple of your best horses over to the hotel. Come on, Bill. We'll need our emergency kits."

The two men hurried into the street. Dern watched their disappearing backs thoughtfully. He was not liking the curious speculation in the brief looks Dr. Royale and his assistant had given him.

He spoke softly to Vince Clayson. "Don't rush those horses over to the hotel too quick. I'm wanting that report on the Springs before he gets away."

"I savvy." The liveryman nodded, pushed into the street.

Dern's look went to the glowering town marshal. "I've no more use for Pinto," he said. "Letting Hill Carnady break Sam Hally from jail."

"That's what he figgered," muttered the town marshal. "Pinto has already lit out for the border."

"You should have emptied your gun into him," grumbled Dern. He reached for his hat. "Let's go over to the hotel. I want to keep tabs on Royale — try and get that report from him."

218

"It's about time I'm getting back and relieve Strawly at the desk," Curly said. "I'll mosey along with you, Boss."

"I've got to get over to the jail," declared the town marshal. He swore feelingly. "All the keys gone and I ain't sure Ike Jones can fix me up new ones."

Ace Roan said it was about time for him to get back to his saloon.

"Or was you wanting me along at the hotel with you?" he asked Dern.

"It won't look good to Royale if I show up with a crowd," Dern decided. "You go on about your business, boys — only keep in touch with me."

The little groups of men had disappeared from the street, he noticed, as accompanied by Curly he made his way to the hotel. Jess Kinner had wasted no time hitting the trail for the ranch with his riders. Jess also had evidently taken most of the other desperados recruited from the border. A fact that did not please the lawyer. He was not liking so many of his hired gunmen to be absent from the town at this moment of impending crisis. Hill Carnady might not be headed for the ranch. He might be dangerously close — looking for Ellen Dunbar. An unpleasant thought that he found disturbing.

A Mexican slouched down the hotel porch steps as they approached — vanished like a wraith into the deepening dusk of an alley.

"Sure looked like Benito — one of Don Julio's fellers," Curly Teel said. "I wonder what he was wanting at the hotel!"

"Go after him!" Dern's voice showed alarm. "I want to know his business here."

"Ain't a chance for me to catch him," protested Curly. "Like as not I'd get a knife in my ribs."

A commotion in the hotel lobby, voices, loud, excited, saved the hotel man from Dern's mounting wrath. The screen door flew open with a crash, and Dr. Royale and Bill Wallace came changing out on the run. The geologist almost collided with Dern at the foot of the steps. He halted, fixed an angry look on the lawyer.

"Sir," he said, in a low, tight voice. "My daughter is safe, and no thanks to you!"

"I'm not responsible for your daughter losing herself in the chaparral," Dern retorted. "I do not care for your manner, Doctor."

"I have just received a message from Don Julio Severa that she is safe at his *casa,*" Royale continued. "It seems, sir, that because of the clothes she was wearing she was mistaken for a certain Miss Dunbar by a scoundrel, in your pay, a man known as Whitey. Only Providence saved her from the wretch."

"I never heard of the man," lied Dern. "I assure you, Doctor that you have been wrongly informed." He hesitated, glanced slyly at Curly Teel. The hotel man was staring with terrified eyes at the gun in the hand of Dr. Royale's tall assistant. No help from Curly at that moment. And Ace Roan was in his saloon, and the town marshal had gone to the jail up on the hill.

Dern's look shifted momentarily down the street. No sign of Vince Clayson coming with the horses the doctor had demanded. Vince was obeying orders not to hurry with the horses only too well.

The lawyer forced himself to keep rising panic from his voice. "I'm terribly sorry about your daughter," he asserted smoothly. "And I don't understand this talk about Miss Dunbar, who happens to be a good friend of mine." He paused. "By the way, Doctor, I'd really like to have your report on that Red Butte Springs property."

"I'm afraid, sir, that I cannot oblige you," Dr. Royale told him frostily. "It is my belief that Miss Dunbar, whose homestead has been burned and who has disappeared, is the rightful owner of Red Butte Springs."

221

He gestured for them to stand aside. "I am going now to get my daughter from Don Julio's *casa*. We'll be leaving on the early morning stage, Dern." He strode across the street. Bill Wallace followed, gun in lifted hand, his expression formidable.

Strawly, the bald, paunchy desk clerk pushed through the screen, followed by a bow-legged cowboy who lounged against the door, an odd glint in hard, watchful eyes. Strawly was making a half-hearted attempt to reach for the gun under his coat. Dern's gesture stopped him.

"It was that Mex hombre, Benito, brought the message," babbled the frightened clerk. "I tried to hold him but he drew a knife — got away."

"You heard what Royale said." Dern's smile was wolfish. "They'll be back — with the girl — and that's just going to suit me fine." His look covered their intent faces. "We'll see to it they don't leave on the early morning stage — or any stage."

"You said a while back that Royale was too important for us to monkey with," Curly Teel reminded uneasily.

"You fool!" exploded the lawyer. "Do you want a rope around your neck? Only one thing we can do, now — make sure none of them leaves Coldwater — *alive.*"

222

For the first time he seemed to notice the hard-faced cowboy idling in the doorway. "Who are you?" he asked, curtly.

"The name's Kansas," answered the cowboy.

Dern studied him thoughtfully, noticed the two guns in low-slung holsters. "What are you doing in this town, Kansas?"

"Looking for a job with some good outfit," Kansas said. "Jess Kinner figgered he could use me, told me to hang around here at the hotel until he was ready to head for the ranch." The cowboy shrugged. "Seems like he went off in a hurry — clean forgot me."

Dern nodded, evidently satisfied. He knew why Jess had left town in such haste. He asked, casually, "Handy with your guns, Kansas?"

"Sure," grinned Kansas. "That's why Kinner figgered to put me on the payroll."

"All right," Dern said. "You're hired." He looked at the horse drooping at the hitch-rail. "That your bronc?"

Kansas nodded. "Sure is."

"Do you know who Steff Hancy is?" queried Dern.

"I sure do. He's town marshal ——"

"All right, Kansas ——" Dern gestured at the hitch-rail. "You fork your bronc and hightail it for the jail. Tell Hancy I want him

223

here at the hotel on the jump, and tell him to bring all the men he can round up, and you get back as quick as you can."

"Sure, Boss ——" Kansas hurried to his horse, swung into his saddle and rode at a lope up the street. Once around the bend that hid him from view, the cowboy turned sharply to the left, sent his horse on the dead run into the trail he knew would take him to the *casa* of Don Julio Severa. Moments were precious.

The killing wolf. I should have used my guns on him when I had the chance. Kansas leaned low in the saddle, spurs urging more speed. *Wish Hill would show up.*

His indignant horse raced on, ears flattened, shod hoofs hammering.

CHAPTER THIRTEEN

Ellen Dunbar lay on the bed, watched the dawn creep into the room. Twenty-four hours now, since she had seen another dawn light the high peaks beyond Coldwater, when Hill Carnady had brought her to the sanctuary behind Don Julio Severa's high walls. She was paying the price of disobedience. Hill Carnady had warned her not to venture into the town. She had acted like a little fool, betrayed Don Julio's fine hospitality, played Delfina a despicable trick. She had only herself to blame for what had happened.

She closed her eyes, tried to shut out the memory of those first horrible moments when she had recognized Bat Savan's face leering back at her from the buckboard's front seat. She had realized then that Oswen Dern was the man responsible for the burning of her homestead — was behind the evil conspiracy that Hill Carnady said was throttling the San Jacinto country. Oswen Dern — the man she had trusted as a good friend! How wise old Captain Carnady had been. He had not trusted Oswen Dern. She recalled the cattleman's gruff comment. *Mighty queer, Dern doesn't seem to know there's a Land Office in Coldwater.*

It came to Ellen, as she lay there on the bed, that Dern had never registered her papers at any Land Office. He probably had filed on the land in his own name — or the name of some paid hireling.

That dreadful drive to the ranch — the stout man by her side, a doctor's black bag at his feet, his hard fingers gripping her arm when she tried to throw herself from the fast-moving buckboard.

"We'll have to put you to sleep, if you don't behave." His meaning was plain enough — a hypodermic — unconsciousness. The thought ended her resistance. She had to keep her senses — her wits.

One thought had sustained her. She might see her brother. It was possible that Oswen Dern had spoken the truth when he said that Dick was still alive, although badly wounded. The man by her side was a doctor and it was obvious that he was needed at the ranch. Perhaps it was Dick who was the patient needing a doctor, or old Captain

Carnady. She could only hope for the best — hope that Dick and Hill's grandfather were still alive.

Her questions failed to elicit any reply from Doc Larny. He would only shake his head. She wondered if such an odious man could really be a doctor. If so, it seemed that whisky had destroyed all decency in him. Some down-and-out physician a man like Dern would find useful. Perhaps a fugitive from the Law.

Twilight was deepening when they reached the ranch. Lamplight glowed from the big, rambling house set back in a grove of great trees. A man, a rifle in his hands, lounged on the veranda. He gave Ellen a curious look as Bat Savan hurried her through a wide door into a hall. He half pushed her towards a stairway, motioned for her to precede him. Her terrified look brought his frightening grin.

"Ain't harmin' you," he said. He touched the arm he wore in a sling. "I ain't saying the same for the feller that got you away from me down there at the Springs."

Ellen sat up on the bed and gazed round this room in which Bat had locked her. The dawn pushing in now revealed that it was a large room. A tall chest of drawers stood against the opposite wall. There was a desk near one of the windows. A pair of worn leather chaps hung from a peg. Spurs dangled from another peg, and there was a gun-rack, now empty. A washstand stood in a corner, with a ewer and basin. There were three chairs, one of them hand-made from manzanita wood. She guessed that it was a man's room — *Hill Carnady's room.* And though she knew that Hill had been away for over a year, she could detect no dust. Somebody had given it loving care. Teresa, his old nurse, Ellen guessed again. She wondered if Teresa might still be alive — in the house.

She got off the bed, shook out her rumpled skirt. She was still wearing the clothes Delfina had provided for her, the gay skirt, the low-cut bodice, the *mantilla* which she kept hugged around her shoulders against the dawn's chill — the red slippers.

Despite her anxiety, her mounting terror, there had been intervals of dozing during the long night. Her young healthy body had demanded some respite from exhausting emotions, and the snatches of sleep had refreshed her, also made her aware of hunger pangs, a distressing thirst. She had seen or heard from nobody since Bat Savan had locked her in the room the previous evening. She began to wonder a bit wildly if they planned to starve her to death.

Hugging the *mantilla* tight over her shoulders, Ellen took a cautious look out of one of the windows. She got a vista of corrals and barns beyond the trees; she also saw a man, leaning against one of the trees opposite the window, a rifle under an arm. If he glimpsed her peering face he chose to ignore her, was apparently intent on the cigarette he was making. She drew back, conscious of a little stab of despair. No hope of escape through that second storey window, even if no guard were there. To climb down that sheer wall was something beyond her. She guessed the real reason for the guard's presence. He was there to prevent an attempt to rescue her. It meant they were on the watch for Hill Carnady. Hill had left Don Julio's *casa* hours before she had stolen away so secretly — so foolishly. His objective would have been the ranch — his grandfather.

The thought sent a thrill through her. Hill was somewhere close. He might even know of the trap that had closed over her — know that she was a helpless prisoner in the ancient ranch house of his ancestors. She had learned much about Hill Carnady since the singing of that Thanksgiving hymn had brought him to her door hardly more than twenty-four hours ago. Hill was too wary to walk into a trap. He knew that caution — cool thinking — the stealth of an Indian on the warpath — spelled the difference between life — or death.

Reviving courage put colour into her cheeks, and there was no hint of fear in her eyes when the door suddenly flung open, revealed Bat Savan's face. A woman stood behind him, plump, grey-haired, compassion, a warning, in dark, kindly eyes. Ellen had seen her before when she had visited Captain Carnady.

"Teresa!" Relief put a lump in Ellen's throat. She found herself wanting to cry. At that moment the old Mexican woman's face was like a glimpse of heaven.

"Si, Señorita ——" Teresa entered the room. She carried a tray, her smile warm, the same hint of warning in her eyes.

"No fool talk," Bat Savan said. He leaned against the door, watchful, his one good hand on the gun in his holster.

"Si, Señor ——" The Mexican woman spoke humbly. She placed the tray on the scarred old desk. "I breeng nize food, *Señorita.* Coffee — water — a leetle milk and cream."

"Thank you, Teresa." Ellen recovered her voice. "I'm starving."

"Pobrecita!" half whispered the Mexican woman. She busied herself, arranging the loaded plates on the desk. A steaming bowl of beef stew, a custard pudding, bread and butter — a pot of coffee, cream, milk — a tall pitcher of water.

Ellen summoned up her little Spanish. *"Gracias,"* she managed, her smile grateful.

Bat Savan, lounging in the doorway, had heard Teresa's whispered ejaculation. "She ain't no poor little one," he jeered. "She'll be lucky she ain't headed for across the border right now." He guffawed, lit the cigarette in his fingers. "Get a move on, you. I'm wanting back to that card game with the Doc and the boys."

Teresa's look warned Ellen to keep her head, ignore the threat about the border. She fluttered hands at a chair. Ellen sat down, took a drink from the water glass. Teresa made soft exclamations, fluttered hands again, hurried on sandalled feet to the washstand and peered into the jug, exclaimed again in Spanish, held the big jug out to Bat.

"You go queek — breeng water," she said.

Bat hesitated, a scowl on his dark face. Teresa ran to him, thrust the ewer into his hands. *"El Señor* Dern say we keep nize care of *Señorita,"* she scolded. "You breeng hot

231

water for her to wash."

Not waiting for the refusal she evidently expected, the Mexican woman went to the bed, began straightening the rumpled cover, turning down the sheet. Bat muttered an oath, turned on his heel, closed the door. They heard the key scrape in the lock — his heavy tread fading down the hall.

The ruse to get rid of the spy was not lost on Ellen. She was out of her chair, running to Hill's old nurse. "Quick — tell me — is my brother, Dick, here —— ?"

Teresa shook her grey head. "He is not here, *Señorita*. He get away with *El Señor McGee*. Their escape make mooch fear weeth those *malo* hombres."

Ellen stared at her, rocked by the news that her brother, supposed to be dying of a gunshot wound, had escaped. The time for questions was all too short. She had to know about Hill's grandfather.

"*El Señor* is still alive," Teresa replied to her anxious inquiry. "*El Señor* 'ave the str-roke, lie in bed." The woman dabbed at wet eyes with her apron. "I 'ave preeten' I 'ate old *Señor* — make those *malo* hombres theenk am frien' of *Señor* Dern . . ." Teresa's gesture was eloquent. "I glad die for heem."

"Oh, Teresa —— !" Ellen kept back her

own tears. It was no time to give way to emotion. She put another question — held her breath for the woman's answer. "Has — has Hill Carnady been here — yet?"

Teresa gave her a searching look, a look that seemed to probe into the depths of her heart. "No, *Señorita.* I 'ave no seen *Hillito.*"

"He is somewhere near us," Ellen confidently told her. Her arms were suddenly around Hill's old nurse. "Teresa — while Hill lives — we can still dare to hope."

"Ave Maria Purissima!" Teresa's dark eyes were again probing, questioning. "I 'ave watch *Hillito* from cradle. *Hillito* ees beeg man — *un cabellero grande* — like old *Señor.*" A smile warmed the Mexican woman's face. "*Señorita* like my *Hillito,* no?"

Ellen nodded her head. "Yes," she said, simply. "Oh, Teresa — he is in great danger! We must pray ——"

The sound of booted feet approached up the hall. Teresa motioned for Ellen to return to the desk — resume her breakfast. "Queek — that *malo hombre* come ——"

The key scraped in the door and Bat Savan pushed into the room, a wooden pail of steaming water dangling from one big hand. He set the pail on the floor near the washstand. "All right, Teresa," he said. "You come along with me. I'm wanting in at the

233

card game with the boys." He turned back to the door, Teresa was seeking another excuse to prolong her talk with Ellen. She gestured indignantly.

"You no breeng the towel — not'ing — no soap ——" she scolded. "You go queek — breeng the towel — the soap!"

Bat glowered, his dark face sulky, flung an impatient look at Ellen's back, and stamped into the hall. Key rasped in lock again. Teresa hastened to the girl's side.

"*Señorita,*" she said in a low voice. "I keep watch for *Hillito* — tell heem you here."

"I'm so afraid they will catch him," worried the girl.

"*Hillito* smar-rt," reassured Teresa. "*Hillito* know *casa* mooch better than those *malo hombres.*" She gave Ellen a confident smile. "They no catch *Hillito.* You watch ——" She gestured at the windows, "— and wait and pray, *Señorita.*" She drew a rosary from inside her dress — kissed it, slid it back from sight. "I pray, too," she added.

The door key turned again and Bat hurried into the room, towels over an arm, a box of soap in his hand. He tossed them into the empty warm basin. "I ain't running no more errands," he grumbled. "Get moving, Teresa ——"

"*Si* ——" The Mexican woman padded

234

into the hall. Ellen's voice halted the renegade in the doorway. "How long are you
going to keep me a — a prisoner here?" she
asked, head turned in an indignant look at
him.

"I reckon that's up to the boss," Bat told
her gruffly.

"Who is your boss?" Ellen wanted to
know.

"I reckon you savvy who's the boss,"
grimaced the man. "You ain't needing me
to tell you his name."

"You mean Oswen Dern is your boss?"

"You sure hit the target plumb centre,
ma'am." Bat hesitated, obviously longing to
divulge exciting news. "He'd have been
along only for some hell busting loose in
town that's kept him back. Jess Kinner
come in late last night with the boys and
says how Hill Carnady's on the loose —
broke Sam Hally from jail." Bat's eyes glit-
tered. "I reckon it was Carnady that put
that slug through my arm when me and you
was heading away from the Springs."

"I'm not telling you who it was," Ellen
retorted.

"Jess and the boys is combing the chaparral for him and old Hally," Bat told her, his
grin wide. "Ain't no chance a-tall for 'em to
git away." The door closed — the key turned

in the lock.

Ellen listened to his fading footsteps — the soft pad of Teresa's sandals. She was conscious of a disturbing giddiness — a mounting terror. Not fear for herself, at that moment. It was the thought of Hill Carnady that sapped the strength from her — filled her with torturing doubts. *Combing the chaparral for him. Ain't no chance for 'em to git away.* The malevolence in Bat's voice — his triumphant grin!

Ellen looked at her plate of stew. Her appetite had vanished. She felt too ill to eat, and yet, food was necessary. Common sense told her that she needed all her strength. Hill Carnady would say, *eat that stew.* She could hear his quiet, resolute voice — recall the courage that was like a living flame in his unafraid blue eyes. The thought of him revived her own waning courage. She must not be found wanting in strength and courage when the moment came. She must eat the good food that Teresa had provided — be ready for any crisis.

She forced her thoughts away from the room that held her prisoner — back to the great *casa* of Don Julio Severa. Her disappearance would have them all dreadfully worried — mystified. She thought miserably of the two Yaqui guards, Justo and Atilano

236

— hoped that old Don Julio would not punish them. Even more disturbing was the thought of Delfina who had been so kind to her.

Ellen determinedly gave her attention to the stew — the hot coffee, tried to stop thinking. She was guilty of so much that was wrong. Betrayal of Don Julio's fine hospitality — Delfina's trust, and disobedience to the wishes of Hill Carnady. He had warned her not to leave the sanctuary he had found for her behind Don Julio's high walls. Her disobedience had done much to increase the dangers confronting Hill Carnady. She could have cried, but tears would not help him, or her.

She made herself finish the beef stew, drink a second cup of coffee, then get out of Delfina's pretty clothes and fill the wash basin from the pail of still warm water. The sponge bath refreshed her. She dressed again, gazed at her face in the small mirror on the chest of drawers, ran fingers through her hair, managed to put some order in the long curls. She was doing all she could to relax nervous tension — strengthen morale, be ready for the moment when Hill Carnady might appear. Teresa had said they must pray. She prayed — prayed for Hill Carnady — his deliverance from the enemies who sought his life.

Finally, she nerved herself to go to one of the windows. The sentry still lounged against the great tree opposite, sitting on his haunches, rifle between knees, cigarette drooping from whiskered lips, hat pulled low over eyes. He was not asleep, though. His head lifted in a quick look at her peering face.

Ellen shifted her gaze to the corrals. Horsemen were streaming in through a gate, off-saddling at the long watering trough under the windmill. Too far for her to recognize faces, but she felt sure that no prisoners were among those men.

Her look returned to the sentry beyond her window. If she had possessed a gun she would have been tempted to send a bullet at him. A quite useless act on her part, Ellen reflected. The death of that guard at her hands would not help Hill Carnady — not with that big corral filling with a score and more border renegades seeking his life. And she possessed no weapon. Bat Savan had been careful about that. No knife or fork, on the tray. Only spoons. The only weapons she could think of were the spurs that dangled from their peg. Spurs fitted for a small boy's boots — Hill Carnady's first boots, she guessed.

Her idling gaze went beyond the sentry, deep into the great grove of trees. Something seemed to stir there, a furtive movement in the bushes.

Her heart stood still, began to pound. She reached blindly for the chair near the desk, almost fell into it, sat there, fighting off the momentary giddiness and berating herself for her weakness. . . . *She must be ready when the time came — not a rubbery-kneed bundle of nerves.*

She forced herself back to the window for another cautious look. She must not let the sentry suspect that something had attracted her attention.

For long moments Ellen gazed intently at the spot where she had seen what could have been a shadow on the sunlit bush — the shadow of a man crouching there. Her eyes began to ache. She must have been mistaken, she decided. What she had glimpsed was the flutter of a bird — some little animal.

Approaching footsteps drew her attention to the garden path below the window. A prickle of fear ran through her as she recognized the newcomer, Kickapoo, one of the trio who had burned the homestead. She guessed that he had come to relieve the guard under the trees.

Eager to overhear their conversation, Ellen carefully slid up the window a few inches.

"About time you got here, Kickapoo. I'm craving breakfast." The sentry's voice, gruff, complaining.

"Would have got here sooner," Kickapoo answered. "Was waiting to hear if the boys picked up that Carnady feller's trail."

"No catch 'em, huh?" The other man was on his feet, rifle tucked under an arm.

"Jess Kinner is one wild man," chuckled Kickapoo. "Just as quick as the boys has et they're heading into the chaparral ag'in for another try."

"They'll pick him up," predicted his companion, turning away. "Him and Sam Hally, both. Well, keep your eyes peeled for 'em, feller."

"We're wasting time, watching the gal's window," Kickapoo said to the man's departing back. "No chance for Carnady to git within a mile of here." He leaned his rifle against the tree and sat down, the huge bole at his back. Ellen drew aside as his face lifted in a look up at her window. She continued her cautious watch, saw a flask suddenly appear in his hand. He took a long swallow. Loud voices, the trample of horses' hoofs in the ranch yard, apparently alarmed

240

him. He hastily returned the flask to a pocket.

Ellen's look went quickly to the big yard. Jess Kinner was losing no time resuming the search for Hill Carnady. Fear again laid clammy fingers on her as she watched the riders stream through the gate — more than a score of them. It did not seem possible that Hill could elude so many. *Combing the chaparral for 'em. . . . Ain't no chance for him to git away. . . .*

Her gaze went back to Kickapoo under the tree. His flask was out again. A forlorn hope stirred in her. If the man continued to tilt that bottle to his mouth his vigilance would be dulled. It was even possible he would fall into a drunken sleep.

She dared another searching scrutiny of the trees beyond the man engrossed with his flask. No movement here in the bushes where she had thought she had seen the shadow of a crouching man. Not even the stirring of branches in that lifeless air.

Despite her resolve to hold fast to courage, her brief glimmer of hope faded. She went slowly to the bed, flung herself face down on the pillow.

CHAPTER FOURTEEN

There were good reasons for Teresa's confident assertion that Hill's enemies would find him difficult to catch. The old ranch house had been his home since the day of his birth, and the surrounding range his playground from the time he could sit his first pony. The barns, the corrals, the canyons and ravines — the creeks and ditches, held no secrets from him. The heritage of the remote southwest had always been warm in him, fired his boyish imagination. He had played all the games, been in turn trapper and mountain man, buffalo hunter, scout — stalking Apache or Comanche, his one companion and playmate the boy his grandfather had rescued from an ambushed wagon-train, the lone survivor of an Apache raid. The boy, too small at the time to tell his name, had always been known as Kansas because Captain Carnady guessed from the signs that the wagon-train hailed from there.

He had grown to young manhood on the ranch, become a top-hand and one of Hill's best friends.

Hill was thinking of Kansas now, as he crouched behind the big catsclaw, alert eyes probing through the trees at the grey walls of the old Carnady ranch house. According to Sam Hally there were rumours that Kansas had been seen in Coldwater. It seemed incredible, though, that Kansas could have betrayed their life-long friendship — thrown in with the ruthless border ruffians now in possession of the ranch. The rumours did not make sense — did not fit into the picture of Kansas, and there was only one answer. Kansas was somewhere not too far away — waiting — and watching for the return of Captain Carnady's grandson. He knew all their boyhood secret hideouts, even the great cave in nearby Cow Creek Canyon where Hill had left the bay horse.

The thought cheered him. When the crisis came, Kansas would be there with his cool head and fast guns. Sam Hally, and Seth McGee, too, that pair of formidable longhorns, and Mat Webster, HC's veteran foreman. Juanito's story of the man he had met near Black Canyon was proof that Mat was still alive. *Tall, and very lean, and had a big nose and a scar on his cheek.* Yes, good, staunch old Mat Webster! Which meant that others of HC's mysteriously missing riders were somewhere close — all of them waiting for Hill Carnady's return. They were depending on him.

He became suddenly aware that his hand was clamped tight over gun butt. He was letting himself get too tense, allowing wishful thinking to distract his attention from the house where his grandfather, if still alive, was a helpless prisoner. For the moment he was on his own, and no immediate help in sight. He must resist senseless speculations, keep his mind functioning smoothly in the job ahead.

He eased to another position, saw with dismay that his shadow slid across the spreading thorny branches. He was instantly prone, but not before he thought he glimpsed a movement in one of the upper windows. His own room, he realized with a heart-sickening jolt. It was quite possible that spying eyes were on the watch up there. Oswen Dern had reason to suspect by now that Hill Carnady was back in the San Jacinto. His hired killers would be on the alert.

The clatter and stamp of horses' hoofs reached him from the ranch yard — men's voices. Hill held his breath, tried to catch the exchange of words the riders were throwing at each other. Too far away. He could only guess that Jess Kinner had arrived with his outfit after long hours of searching for him and Sam Hally. Sam's escape from jail would have sent Oswen Dern into a frenzy; and the horses ridden into Coldwater by Dr. Royale and his assistant would have been recognized. Dern would have soon realized that Topaz and Pedro had failed to ambush Captain Carnady's grandson up on the Borrego rimrock. He could visualize the lawyer's consternation — the immediate exodus of Jess Kinner's riders from Coldwater. No lynch party now, but a grim search for Sam Hally and Hill Carnady. Oswen Dern would be very certain of the identity of the man who had rescued Ellen Dunbar from the men who had put the torch to her house and barns. He would guess, too, the name of the red-headed Mexican who had broken Sam Hally and Juanito Sanchez from jail in time to thwart a lynching party; and he would guess, too, who had supplied Dr. Royale and Bill Wallace with the horses and saddles once used by Topaz and Pedro.

Hill speculated briefly about Dr. Royale, wondered if the great mining expert had told Dern about the fabulous wealth of copper under the red butte that gave the springs its name. He hoped he had said enough to make Dr. Royale decide not to tell Dern about his discovery. A difficult situation, though, for the mining expert, and more dangerous than he might realize. An attempt to fool Oswen Dern could easily lead to a mysterious disappearance in the chaparral of the San Jacinto. It would never be known what had happened to Dr. Royale, his daughter — and his assistant.

The crunch of bootheels broke into Hill's sombre thoughts. He peered under a clawing branch of the bush that hid him from view, saw a short, thick-set man approaching the huge tree opposite his bedroom windows. He saw too, another man appear from the far side of the tree's great bole, a rifle under his arm.

Hill was conscious of a cold prickle down his spine. He had not been aware of that armed guard so snugly concealed from view. He blessed the memory of those boyhood days when he used to play *Apache* with Kansas. They would take turns stalking the ranch house. Sometimes he would be the ranchman, on guard with his make-believe Sharps buffalo gun, with Kansas crawling through the bushes, scalping knife in hand. The tree was not so big, then, but big enough to cover his small lean frame until Kansas slid from the bushes into the sight of his Sharps rifle. A lot of fun in those days, but now the stalking was in grim earnest, and he was the stalker — with life or death the stake.

He strained his ears to catch what the men were saying . . . *heading into the chaparral ag'in for another try . . . they'll pick him up . . . wasting time watching the gal's window. . . .*

Hill's heart turned over. He looked up at the window, again, thought he saw a movement there — a momentary glimpse of a face . . . *the gal's window. . . .* He knew of only one girl who could be a prisoner up in that room, Ellen Dunbar, supposed to be safely behind Don Julio's well-guarded walls, her presence there unknown to her enemies.

He continued to watch and listen. The newcomer was talking again, his voice loud as he called after his departing fellow-renegade. *No chance for Carnady to git within a mile of here. . . .* The man leaned his rifle against the tree and was lost from view now on the far side of the great bole. Hill guessed that he had settled down to take it easy while he kept watch on the window. He realized, too, that it was hopeless for the girl to escape from that second storey window, which meant that the watch was really for him. Oswen Dern would correctly suspect that he would make an attempt to rescue Captain Carnady, and would soon learn that Ellen Dunbar was also a prisoner in the ranch house.

Voices again reached him from the ranch yard as he lay there, considering what to do. The stamp of shod hoofs, the creak of saddle leather. Jess Kinner and his riders were leaving to continue their relentless search for himself and Sam Hally.

He waited, reining hard on his impatience, until the sounds faded into the distance. A hush settled over the place. Only the bellow of one of the milk cows, calling for her calf, the crow of a rooster — the cackle of a hen telling the world she had laid an egg — the clatter of pans in the kitchen. Hill thought of Teresa. If still alive she would never leave Captain Carnady. Juanito had not been able to give him news of her. If he could only get into the house he would soon know if his old nurse were still alive, find out what had happened to his grandfather. It was going to be difficult to get to his grandfather. He was not even sure that the old cattleman was alive. Teresa would know, though, and he knew of a secret entrance into the cellar. He and Kansas had made it with his grandfather's indulgent permission during those boyhood days. There was a rope ladder they had fashioned and always kept carefully hidden in a cunningly-concealed cache behind some adobe bricks. Once in the cellar he could easily climb into the hall between the kitchen and the dining-room.

He found himself again speculating about the girl who from the lookout's words was evidently a prisoner in his bedroom. The only answer was Ellen Dunbar, but how she could possibly have fallen into Oswen Dern's hands was a mystery hard to explain. He had warned her not to leave the protection of Don Julio's *casa*. It was difficult to believe that she would risk showing herself in Coldwater.

Eyes alert for any movement beyond the big tree, Hill scoured his mind for an answer that would explain why Ellen Dunbar was a prisoner up in that bedroom a scant fifty yards from where he crouched behind the big catsclaw. He was sure that the face he had briefly glimpsed was a girl's face — Ellen's face. He could arrive at only one possible solution. Ellen had not realized that Dern was responsible for the raid that had left her homestead in smouldering ruins. He himself had not been really sure about Dern until his talk with Sam Hally. Ellen naturally considered Dern still her good friend, decided she must have a talk with him, tell him what had happened — ask his help to find her missing brother. She had managed to slip away from the *casa* and go to Dern's office — innocently walked like a fly into the spider's web.

The stillness continued, touched only by the intermittent bawls of the cow calling for her calf. It was evident that Jess Kinner was using his entire outfit for a final combing of the hills and canyons and mesas. The ranch house was practically deserted, except for perhaps two or three men. A couple would be in the house, making sure that his grandfather and Ellen did not leave their rooms. The man he had seen relieved from his post below the window would likely be asleep in the bunkhouse after his night's watch. The immediate job would be to take the lookout man now on guard under the window by surprise, silence him — kill him if necessary.

Hill drew the Colt .45 from its holster, eyed it thoughtfully. That long steel barrel could crack a man's skull like an egg shell. All he needed was to get close enough — swing hard.

He made a quick run to another bush, his feet hardly a whisper in the sun dried grass still sodden from the previous evening's thundershower. Yard by yard, he made the approach, reached a shrub close to the tree. A movement there held him motionless, gun ready; and then he recognized the sound — the gurgle of liquor, twice repeated; followed by a muttered oath.

"Damn if she ain't empty," he heard the lookout mutter. "Should have had me another pint along." There was a swish in the bushes, a tinkle of glass as the discarded flask shattered against a rock. "I sure could take a *siesta* right now."

It was plain from the man's voice that he was drunk, his vigilance dulled. Hill turned the thought over in his mind. It was not going to be difficult to remove him from the scene, not even necessary to lay the steel barrel of his .45 over the man's skull. He wanted to get him away on his own feet instead of having to drag him senseless, or dead, into the bushes. The man could give him valuable information. Also his complete disappearance would mystify the others if chance should find him missing from his post. They would probably think that he had decided to say *adios* to the affair and hit the trail for some safer place south of the border. He doubted, though, that the man's disappearance would become known until

251

somebody came to relieve him, or Jess Kinner returned, or — and this last possibility put ice into Hill's eyes, the arrival of Oswen Dern from Coldwater.

His look went up briefly to the bedroom window. Nothing showed there, now. He wondered unhappily what to do about Ellen. Her presence there was an unexpected blow, added to the difficult problem of getting his grandfather away. His time would be all too short.

A snore came from the other side of the big tree. Hill wasted no more moments. Soft-footed as a panther, he slipped round the tree, plucked the gun from the dozing man's holster, stepped back from arm's reach and nudged one of the outstretched booted feet. Kickapoo came awake, hand reached for the gun no longer there.

He gazed up, mouth open, horror, disbelief, in shocked eyes. Hill said softly, "Just one word, and I'm killing you." He motioned with one of the guns for the frightened man to get to his feet. Kickapoo obeyed, and at another gesture from Hill, went stumbling on shaky legs into the grove. Hill holstered his own .45, snatched up the Winchester leaning against the tree, and followed close on his heels, prodding his back with the rifle. In less than a minute they

252

were down in a ditch that ran across the grove and was used for flooding the trees. Storm waters still flowed down it from Cow Creek Canyon. The stream was hardly more than a foot deep, but enough to cover their tracks in the event of an unexpected too-soon search.

They splashed along for a couple of hundred yards, Hill prodding his prisoner along with the rifle. The shock had considerably sobered Kickapoo, and the press of the gun on his spine put the fear of death in him, and surprising speed into his legs.

They left the ditch and turned into a trail that twisted up a shallow gulch. A voice spoke softly from behind a boulder.

"Señor ——"

Old Pablo's voice! Sheer astonishment froze Hill in his tracks, and taking advantage of his momentary inattention, Kickapoo plunged from the trail, disappeared in the brush. Almost instantly another voice spoke, and for all its youth there was death in the sharp-flung command to halt. Juanito's voice, and in another moment he appeared, his gun prodding Kickapoo back on to the trail.

Pablo appeared from behind his boulder, a hint of apprehension on his gnarled brown face. Hill guessed the thought that troubled the old Mexican. He said, gratefully, in Spanish, "I am glad you disobeyed me, Pablo, and followed my trail."

"We go where you go," Pablo told him. "Death rides your trail, and we would be at your side."

"Gracias, amigo," smiled Hill. "I am needing your help." He suddenly turned with a menacing gesture on Kickapoo. "Talk fast," he said. "Is Captain Carnady still alive?"

Kickapoo nodded. "Sure . . . kinder sick, though ——" He rolled frightened eyes at them. "I ain't never harmed him," he mumbled.

"Who is the girl up in that room?" Hill asked him.

"Some gal the boss sent in from Coldwater last evening," Kickapoo answered sullenly. "I ain't knowing much about her."

"Ellen Dunbar?"

"I reckon so." Kickapoo licked dry lips. "Leastways, that's what Bat Savan calls her."

"How many men in the house now?" Hill asked him.

"I ain't knowing for sure. Mebbe two or three — a couple more in the bunkhouse."

Hill put another question, although he was sure he already knew the answer. "What about Seth McGee and the Dunbar girl's brother?"

"They got away from us ——" Kickapoo's weathered face took on a grey look as he recalled the escape. "I'd sooner tangle with a wildcat than that McGee hombre."

Hill made a shrewd guess. "You were on guard when they escaped?"

The man nodded. "Left me hawg-tied in the granary."

"There was talk that young Dunbar accidentally shot himself — was dying."

Kickapoo shook his head. "That's what Bat Savan told the gal the night we was ——" He broke off, his round face a quivering mask of fear as he saw the cold rage in Hill's eyes.

"So you are one of the three men who burned the Dunbar place — shot their horses — tried to abduct Miss Dunbar." There was death in Hill's quiet voice. "Where are the other two men — Bat Savan and Whitey?"

"I ain't knowing where Whitey is at." Kickapoo's voice was hardly more than a hoarse whisper. "Bat — he's in the house — keeping tabs on the gal."

"I should kill you here and now," Hill told him.

A knife was suddenly in Juanito's hand. "I keel heem," he said. The young Mexican's smile was wicked.

The renegade was suddenly down on his knees. "Mister," he babbled, "turn me loose, and I'm riding away from here so fast my dust won't never catch up with me this side of the Panhandle."

"I'm leaving it to the Law to deal with you," Hill told the man. "I'm thinking the Law will hang you, along with Bat Savan and a few others."

Juanito regretfully sheathed his knife, disappointment plain on his face. Hill looked at him, shook his head. "You heard what I said, Juanito. Always remember that the Law is on our side."

"*Si, Señor* ——" The young Mexican gestured. "You are my Law," he said in Spanish.

Hill was in desperate haste to get back to the house before Jess Kinner and his riders returned. Only two or three men there, according to Kickapoo. He had planned to take his prisoner to the secret cave in Cow Creek Canyon, leave him securely tied up there. The unexpected appearance of his Mexican friends meant the saving of precious minutes. Neither of them knew where to find the secret hide-out, but he could safely leave his captive, tied hand and foot, with old Pablo. He would take the more agile younger Mexican back to the house with him. He could use Juanito's sharp eyes and ears — his ready knife.

"We need a rope," he said. "Are your horses close?"

"*Si, Señor* ——" Pablo turned away, came to an abrupt standstill at a gesture from Juanito.

"*Señor,*" whispered the youth. "Men come ——" He gestured again, up the trail that led into Cow Creek Canyon.

Hill was instantly in motion, rifle prodding his prisoner into the brush. A backward glance told him that Pablo and Juanito had disappeared into the concealing willows. He, too, now, could hear the approaching hoof thuds. Several horsemen — some of Jess Kinner's riders still on their relentless search for him. A shout from his prisoner would bring them on their quarry with blazing guns.

The thought was unbearable. Discovery now meant the finish for all of them — his grandfather, Ellen — himself. Only immediate action could prevent complete disaster. No use warning his prisoner to keep quiet. The man would not give up such a chance for freedom. He, too, now heard the approaching riders, would guess who they were. His lifted head, the tensing of the cords in his neck, said he was summoning the nerve to let out the yell that would bring his friends on the run.

Hill shifted the Winchester's muzzle from Kickapoo's spine, swung the steel barrel hard against his temple. The man's beginning shout faded into a low moan as he fell, limp — unconscious.

For a long moment, Hill crouched behind a nearby bush, the rifle ready in his hands. If it came to the worst, he would shoot to kill. And somewhere close would be old Pablo and Juanito. Their guns, too, would take toll. They still had a fighting chance, now that Kickapoo was unable to send a warning shout.

A hush up on the trail told him the riders had halted. He heard a low murmur of voices and guessed that the telltale tracks of booted feet had been noticed. There was something familiar about those voices.

Hill got to his feet, hardly believing his ears.

"Sure looks fresh to me." Kansas, always laconic, chary with words.

"That was his bay horse in the cave — the one he was riding when we met him at Red Butte Springs." The Scot's voice of Dr. Royale's assistant.

"Four men make those track." Two voices chiming together like one, the Yaqui twins,

Justo and Atilano.

A great load rolled from Hill's shoulders. Not enemies, seeking his life, but friends in a time of need. A deep gratitude waved through him, put a tightness in his throat that held him silent for a moment.

He managed a husky shout, "Hi, there, Kansas, you old son-of-a-gun! Don't shoot! You've got me."

He pushed through the bushes into the trail, stood there, breathing a bit hard, the relief in his eyes something they would never forget.

"Jess Kinner's outfit is looking for me," he said. "I thought you were some of his riders." His look went to Kansas. "I've been hoping you'd show up, cowboy. We've got work to do."

Bill Wallace said, "Justo and Atilano say there are four of you here. Where are the others?"

Hill gestured at Pablo and Juanito, watching from the big boulder, their dark faces without expression, bleak as the brown hills at their backs. "The fourth man," he said in Spanish, "lies where I left him." His hand lifted in another gesture below the trail. "Get him over to our cave, Kansas, and leave Pablo to keep him safe for the hangman." He gave the old Mexican a grim smile. *"Sabe usted, amigo mio?"*

"Si, Señor ——" Pablo's eyes were smouldering coals under his bristling thatch of white brow. "Those *malo* hombre no get loose from me," he added in his slow, careful English, for the benefit of the tall young Scotsman.

Kansas said, "Listen, Hill. We got news ——" He looked at Bill Wallace. "You tell him, mister ——"

"Dr. Royale's daughter, Lucy was out painting ——" Wallace paused, a hint of chagrin in his eyes. "You had us fooled, when you passed the hotel. None of us guessed you were not the Mexican you seemed to be."

Hill nodded. "Yes, I remember — but let's not waste time ——"

"A rather nasty affair for her," Wallace continued. "It seems that a man known as Whitey followed her, believing that she was Miss Dunbar. . . ." He gave the Yaquis a grateful look. "These men arrived in time to save her life, and thinking she *was* Miss Dunbar, took her back to Don Julio's *casa* where of course she was able to correct the mistake."

"Those *malo* hombre ver' dead," Justo told Hill.

"Bussard peek hees bone," Atilano said.

"A narrow escape ——" Wallace paused. "We are very grateful to them, and to you, Mr. Carnady for your help down there at Red Butte Springs."

"Miss Dunbar is a prisoner here, and my grandfather," Hill said. "Quick — what is this news Kansas says you have? We've got to work fast — before Kinner and his gang get back."

"Dern was alarmed when Dr. Royale refused to give him a report on Red Butte," Bill Wallace told him.

"We had hurried over to Don Julio's *casa* to bring Lucy back to the hotel, planning to leave on the early stage this morning. Kansas learned that Dern was not going to let us leave town, now or ever. He warned us in time, at the risk of his own life."

Kansas shrugged as he met Hill's inquiring look. "I got Dern to thinkin' I was one of his bunch," he drawled. "The coyote sent me high tailin' to the jail to get Steff Hancy over to the hotel with some fellers to lay for 'em when they got back with the gal. I headed for the *casa* instead."

"In short," Wallace went on, "Dern is like a madman, swears he will get us if it means burning Don Julio's place to the ground. We also learned that Miss Dunbar had fallen into his hands and that he had sent

261

her to the ranch. It seemed best to find you at once — let you know the situation. Don Julio insisted that we take these Yaquis to pick up your trail. Best trackers in the world."

"Don Julio said they can follow a wood tick in the dark," Kansas told Hill in Spanish with a grin at the Yaqui twins.

"It is true," Justo declared.

"It is true," echoed Atilano. He crossed thumb and forefinger. "*Por esta cruz* — we follow your trail — or Don Julio take our ears."

Bill was silent, his face thoughtful. The arrival of these men offered attractive immediate action, a heaven-born chance to rescue his grandfather and Ellen Dunbar from the ranch house before the return of Jess Kinner and his more than score riders.

He studied them. Bill Wallace, the big Scotsman, a rifle in saddle-boot, a gun in his holster — a fighting man. Kansas, whose courage he well knew — the two guns in his holsters. The Yaqui twins — born fighting men, and loyal old Pablo and young Juanito. Six good friends, worth a dozen and more of Oswen's Dern's hired desperados.

He made a mental subtraction. Pablo must be left behind to guard Kickapoo in the cave, a safer place to leave his valuable prisoner. Also he wanted the horse he had left hidden there. He was suddenly aware of Bill's voice, speaking words that instantly veered his racing thoughts in another direction.

"Here's a bit more news you'll be interested to hear, Carnady. One of Don Julio's men, Benito, picked it up a few minutes before we left the *casa*. Dern is on his way to the ranch — planned to leave town early this morning."

Kansas was watching Hill, a gleam in his hard eyes. "Only one road to the ranch, Hill," he said softly. "He'll be drivin' in his buckboard, with mebbe three or four fellers ridin' scout."

Hill nodded that he understood. Once Dern was in his hands, the end was in sight. No need, then, to worry about his grandfather or Ellen Dunbar. Not even Jess Kinner, or any of them, would dare lift a hand against the old cattleman or the girl. They would scatter like dry autumn leaves in the wind. It could mean a desperate fight, though, if Kinner and his men made contact with their boss. He longed for Sam Hally and Seth McGee, and Mat Webster — and those others of the old HC outfit.

"Where are they, Kansas?" he asked.

Kansas understood. His face went bleak.

"Six of 'em was killed," he said. "Shot to death in the corral. I ain't knowing where the rest of 'em are."

"I think I know where Mat Webster is hiding out," Hill told him. His thoughts were racing again, Don Julio was needing help. His walls were high and strong, his retainers loyal and brave; but Dern was a desperate man, faced with ruin, even death, unless his schemes triumphed. He could wipe out the entire Severa household, leave the *casa* in ashes, claim that Don Julio had traitorously planned an uprising of the local Mexicans. The old hidalgo had always been indulgently regarded as a harmless irreconcilable hangover from the Mexican War. Dern could make the story sound plausible. It was entirely possible that he had already sent out a call for a gathering of his border renegades. And once he had removed the two Carnadys from the scene, and the remnants of HC's old outfit, his word would be law in the San Jacinto. The fact that he was hurrying to the ranch boded ill for old Captain Carnady and Ellen Dunbar. They were due for his personal and deadly attention. He was, of course, confident that Jess Kinner and his riders would soon flush Hill Carnady and his friends from their hiding places — put an end to them.

Hill could find only one answer for the immediate problem. "Juanito," he said, "You get moving fast to Black Canyon, find Sam Hally, tell him that Don Julio is needing him in town on the jump — all of the old outfit he can round up. *Sabe usted?*"

"*Si, Señor* ——" Juanito was already on the run towards his concealed horse. "I ride like hell, *Señor.*"

Hill said to Kansas, "You know where the road from Coldwater loops this side of Hell Pass?"

"I savvy, Boss!" The cowboy's voice was grimly exultant. "You're sure fixin' to catch us a wolf!"

"You've guessed it," Hill said. "The place is a ready-made trap — and we'll be the teeth." He was looking at Bill Wallace. "Getting hold of Dern will mean the end of his days in the San Jacinto. There'll be shooting, though, if we run into Jess Kinner's gang."

Wallace straightened in his saddle. "Carnady," he said, "you can count me in. Let's ride!"

CHAPTER FIFTEEN

The grade slowed the fast-stepping black Morgans to a walk that made Oswen Dern fidget in the rear seat of the buckboard, a special three-seater job built to his order. Facing him from the opposite seat were Ace Roan and the big-paunched Strawly, guns in their belts, rifles between knees, watchful eyes on the receding road. Vince Clayson, who was driving, occupied the front seat with Curly Teel by his side. Like the two men behind him, Curly was heavily armed, a rifle between his knees.

Dern glanced over his shoulder at the two riders who followed the buckboard, rifles in saddle-boots, guns in holsters. His rear guard; and far ahead, now nearing the summit, two more armed riders, keeping vigilant watch for a possible ambush. He never ventured far without these wary-eyed, quick-shooting men. Even Hill Carnady would find it difficult to waylay him. Four armed riders guarding front and rear, and four good fighting men in the buckboard, not counting himself.

The progress up the long grade was making him restless. He called out, impatiently, "Faster, Vince! Use your whip!"

"I'm handlin' this team the best I know," Vince retorted. "This here rig is carrying a load and we don't want 'em to give out on us."

"Hell Pass ain't no race track," Ace Roan reminded. "Don't worry, Boss. We'll roll fast enough down the Loop."

Dern made no comment, nervously fumbled a small silver flask from under his linen dust coat. He shook his head, thrust the flask back. Whisky could do him no good, relieve his taut nerves, banish the fears that had ridden him ever since the truth about Kansas had burst on him like a bombshell. The cowboy had completely wrecked his plot to trap Dr. Royale and his people in the hotel, force the mining expert to deliver his report on Red Butte Springs.

Mounting panic had brought the decision to leave Coldwater and make for the ranch. Most of his men were with Jess Kinner, searching for Hill Carnady and the remnants of HC's old outfit. Overnight his position had become dangerously vulnerable.

Anything could happen, especially if Don Julio should realize his opportunity; and Dr. Royale, in his anger, would be sure to do considerable urging. The old *caballero's* more than twenty loyal retainers could easily seize the town.

The lawyer reached for his flask again, this time took a long drink. He had sent Steff Hancy to Coyote Wells to round up all the desperados he could find in that border town. If Steff got back in time he could hold Don Julio's Mexicans behind their walls until Jess Kinner arrived with his outfit. Their combined forces could then easily put an end forever to Don Julio and all those who had taken refuge with him.

Another thought made Dern squirm in his seat. It was entirely possible that the town marshal might decide to say *adios* to Coldwater and the threat of a hangman's noose — keep going until he was south of the border.

Dern was suddenly aware of an impotent rage in him as he sensed the furtive curiosity in the eyes of the two men facing him from the opposite seat. They suspected his misgivings and were doing some uneasy thinking for themselves. He could not trust any of them — they would all desert him at the first sign of disaster. All of them — Ace

Roan, Strawly, Vince Clayson — Curly Teel. Hardened desperados who would think only of their own necks.

He thought of Jess Kinner. Perhaps the foreman had caught up with Hill Carnady and Sam Hally, and Jess would take no prisoners. He would leave them in the chaparral where he found them. He hoped that Jess would be back at the ranch when he arrived. He would send Jess and his riders on the jump to Coldwater to take care of Don Julio — Royale, and all the others in the *casa*. Jess could do it, even without Steff Hancy's help. Only old Carnady and the Dunbar girl would be left, and they were safe in the ranch house. It was not too late to force Captain Carnady to sign the deed that would give him possession of the ranch. Once he had the coveted deed he would leave it to Doc Larny to take care of the old man.

He speculated briefly about Ellen Dunbar. She was a good-looking girl, and sensible. He had always hoped that she could be persuaded to become the wife of Coldwater's leading citizen. She would do much to save her brother's life. He had warned Bat Savan not to let her know about Dick Dunbar's escape, and he had told Jess to take Dick alive if he ran into the boy. Dick

269

would be a valuable hostage — a telling argument when it came to a show down with Ellen Dunbar.

Vince Clayson's voice broke into his half-crazed reflections.

"We're just about over the hump, Boss. I reckon I'll let the team get their wind back before we drop down the Loop. This Hell Pass grade is a damn long pull."

The two advance riders had been waiting on the summit. Vince gave them a yell. "All right, fellers — keep moving. We'll be right on your tail."

One of the men waved a hand and in a moment they dropped from view. The buckboard team dug in shod hoofs for a final scramble up the steep incline and came to a willing halt on the cliff-girded summit. The horses were breathing hard, their black coats sweat-lathered.

Vince looked at the little spring that welled from one of the granite cliffs. "I'll give 'em a mouthful of water," he said, and climbed from his seat.

"You're wasting time," Dern fretted. "Keep going, Vince."

The liveryman gave him a surly glance. "These Morgans is good stock," he said. "I ain't killin' 'em for nobody." He picked up a battered bucket crowded under a rock against the wind and proceeded to fill it. The two rear riders came up, swung from saddles and stood waiting for their turn with the bucket.

From where he sat in the buckboard, Dern glimpsed the advance riders disappearing around the first bend below the summit. He knew that from here on Hell Pass was an almost one-way road that went down in a series of sharp loops between towering cliffs. Once out of the canyon the road twisted through the willow brakes of the San Jacinto River for some five miles, to the gate of the horse pasture, less than a mile from the ranch house.

He sat back in his seat, lighted a cigar. No need to worry about running into Hill Carnady, who, if not already dead, was too busy eluding Jess Kinner's relentless search to think of keeping watch on the road from Coldwater. In fact, Hill would not suspect that Oswen Dern was on his way to the ranch. Nor was it possible for him to get into the house unseen, attempt to rescue his grandfather. Too many guards on the alert.

Dern smiled at the two men opposite him, drew out his flask. "Have a drink, boys. I'm thinking we're still sitting pretty."

Ace Roan grinned back at him, took a long drink, handed the flask to Strawly. "I'm

271

bettin' the same way, Boss," the saloon man chuckled.

Strawly took his swallow, handed the flask over his shoulder to Curly Teel in the front seat. Curly drank, looked inquiringly at Vince who was letting the blacks drink sparingly from the bucket. Vince shook his head. "I've got my own flask," he said.

The hotel man hesitated, tilted the flask for a second drink. Dern said sharply, "Hand it back, Curly. I can use what's left."

"I should have brought my own," Curly grumbled as he passed the flask over his shoulder.

"There's plenty more at the ranch house," Dern assured him. "Wait until we finish with this business and you can drink a barrel of it for all I care." He took a small swallow, repocketed the flask, puffed on his cigar. "Let's get going, Vince," he called out.

Vince paused for a minute, drank deep from his own flask before climbing back into his seat. Dern spoke to the riders who were watering their horses.

"Wait until we get round the first bend," he told them. "Keep a sharp eye behind you at each turn."

"We savvy, Boss," one of the men assured him. "Ain't nobody can sneak up on us from behind."

His companion looked up at the ribbon of blue sky above the sheer cliffs. "Ain't nobody can sneak down on us from up yonder."

Vince gave the blacks their heads and the buckboard began its descent of the steep grade. Shod hoofs clattered on the stony road-bed, washed of its dirt covering by the recent storms. The team's stride lengthened under the push of the careening vehicle and brakes began to squeal under the press of the driver's booted foot. Dern found himself clutching the seat rails.

"Not so fast!" he yelled. "You'll run us into the cliff!"

Vince threw him an incensed look over his shoulder. "Just a while back you was bawlin' for me to go faster." He managed to slow the team to a walk for the first hairpin turn.

Ace Roan, watching up the grade as they made the turn, said, "The fellers is waiting up on the summit like you told 'em to, Dern."

They had a clear view now down to the next bend some two hundred yards away. The advance riders had already disappeared round the turn.

Dern frowned. "They should keep us in sight," he complained. "They're getting too far ahead of us."

"I reckon they hear us coming, all right," Vince reassured him. "Quit your worryin'." The wheels were spinning again, the brakes squealing. The buckboard swayed and jolted. Vince bore down more heavily on the foot brake. He knew that the second bend must be taken at a slow walk. The cliffs there drew in dangerously close. A miscalculation could mean a smashed wheel.

Ace Roan was watching up the grade as they crawled round the turn. "The fellers ain't showed up at the first bend," he said. "They're sure taking their time, following u."

Dern hardly heard him. He was gazing down grade. His advance riders were nowhere in sight. They had already disappeared round the third bend.

"Vince ——" He spoke quietly, not wishing to betray his growing uneasiness. "Let's wait a minute — give the boys behind us a chance to catch up."

Vince drew the team to a halt. "Mighty queer they don't keep up with us," he grumbled.

Curly Teel's eyes were fixed on the third bend below them. "I'm thinking it's more queer them fellers ahead keep movin' so fast. We ain't seen 'em since they left the

274

summit."

Dern was studying the sheer cliffs that walled them in. There was not enough room to turn round. It was either stay where they were or continue down the grade. He was reluctant to make the third turn without first receiving the agreed signal from his advance riders.

"Curly," he said. "You go down and take a look round the bend. Give us a yell if you see the boys waiting. Ace, you head back up the grade and take a look round the first loop and see what's holding the other men back."

Ace climbed from his seat. "You would pick on me to climb that damn grade," he muttered.

Curly made no comment. He slid from the front seat, and rifle under his arm, strode down the road. It was plain that he was pleased not to have been chosen for the uphill climb to the first bend.

Ace disappeared into the hairpin curve immediately in their rear. Strawly gave Dern a grin. "He ain't liking to make that climb."

"You go and stand watch in the turn," Dern told him. "Stand just far enough around so Ace can see you to signal if the boys are coming from the summit."

Strawly heaved himself into the road,

waddled back to the hairpin turn. For all his clumsy, big-paunched body, the hotel desk clerk was fast with his guns, perhaps the most ruthless of the renegades Dern had gathered round him.

"Seems like you act awful scary, Boss," commented Vince from his driver's seat.

Dern ignored him. He was watching Curly, now approaching the third bend below. Vince was watching, too. He said softly, "He's round the bend — but he ain't sent us a yell that he sees 'em."

Both men turned their heads like puppets on the same string and looked back at the turn behind them. They could see Strawly, standing where the loop made its sharp angle to the left. He was gazing intently up the grade, and even from where they sat in the buckboard they sensed that what he saw, or did not see, was puzzling him. He was suddenly hurrying towards them, a perturbed look on his big, red face.

"Ace went round the upper loop ——" Strawly's eyes were bulging. "He ain't sending any signal, though, and he's sure had plenty time."

Dern and Vince exchanged uneasy looks, and Vince said gruffly, "Something awful wrong up there on the summit Boss. Let's get movin' — and fast."

276

"That's what I say." Strawly scrambled into the front seat, laid his rifle across knees. "No sense for us to wait here."

"No!" Rage and fear made Dern's voice a hoarse whisper. His hand slipped under the dust coat, came out with a derringer. "Keep your team at a standstill, Vince, or I'll send a bullet into your spine."

Vince stiffened under the press of the deadly little gun against his backbone. "You're crazy," he mumbled. "Like Strawly says, there's no sense for us to wait here. Only way out is down the loop."

"There's trouble down there, too." Dern kept the little double-barrelled pistol tight against the liveryman's back. "Something has happened to Curly, or he'd have given us a yell to come ahead."

Strawly and Vince sat very still, waited for him to continue, or perhaps for a chance to knock the derringer from his hand. It was Strawly who broke the silence.

"You ain't thinking it's Jess Kinner and his outfit that's got us bottled up — that mebbe Jess has throwed in with old Cap Carnady?"

"Not Jess Kinner," Dern said. "It's Hill Carnady that has us bottled up."

"Hill Carnady hell," scoffed Vince. "He ain't got the outfit to pull off a play like

277

this." His fingers were wrapped hard over the reins. "Take that gun out of my back and let's get rollin'."

"No!" repeated Dern. "We've got to figure this thing out before we start rolling."

"There's not enough room for us to turn round and head back up the grade," argued Strawly. "Looks like there's plenty trouble up on the summit, too — Ace not comin' back." He paused, a cunning glint in his eyes. "And I reckon no goat, can climb them cliffs. Take a look, Boss ——"

As Dern instinctively looked up at the blue ribbon of sky framed by the sheer canyon walls, Strawly turned in his seat and made a lightning grab for the gun. He was not quite fast enough. Dern's bullet took him between the eyes, and startled by the gunfire, the black Morgans jumped into a dead run down the grade. The sudden forward jerk hurled the lifeless Strawly over the wheels and threw Dern against the back of his seat, the derringer dropping from his hand as he grasped frantically at the seat rails to save himself from following the dead man into the roadway.

Vince Clayson fought desperately to slow the team for the sharp turn ahead. The buckboard was careening dangerously and every moment threatened to crash against the side of the cliff. Reins wrapped round big hands, foot clamped hard on brake, Vince managed to regain some control of the runaways. They slammed round the hairpin curve, the buckboard swaying precariously. Another bend loomed a short distance ahead. By now the pull of the reins, the drag of brakes, had slowed the horses to a trot. As they slithered round the turn the cliffs drew apart. Two men blocked the road, rifles in their hands. The team came to a halt and a third man appeared from the side of the road, seized their bridles.

Dern cowered in his seat as the other two men approached the buckboard. One of them was Dr. Royale's assistant, Bill Wallace. His companion had red in his hair and wore the clothes of a Mexican vaquero, only Oswen Dern knew that he was not a Mexican. He knew with sickening horror that he was face to face with Hill Carnady.

Vince made no attempt to reach for the gun in his holster. He climbed down from his seat, lifted both hands above his head.

"You, too, Dern," Hill said.

Dern seemed unable to move. He cringed in the seat, lip lifted in the snarl of a cornered wolf.

Vince looked at him, hatred in his eyes. "Look out, Mister," he said to Hill. "He's got a derringer laying on the floor. He used one bullet to kill Strawly back in the Pass. There's another bullet he figgered to use on me."

"Gracias," thanked Hill. He reached inside the buckboard, snatched up the derringer. "All right, Dern. Climb down or I'll pull you out by the neck."

Dern obeyed, leaned for support against a rear wheel. He was looking now at a little group standing in the bushes off the roadside. His two advance riders and Curly Teel, hands tied behind their backs, a rope twisted round their ankles and made fast to the stump of a piñon. Vince Clayson was looking, too. The liveryman threw them a mirthless grin, stood very still while Hill removed the gun from his holster.

"Mister," he said earnestly. "I'm fed up with Dern. Turn me loose and I'll ride so far from these parts a postcard won't catch up with me in a thousand years."

"I'm holding you for now," Hill told him. "Keep on thinking that way and you'll make a good witness for the Law."

Kansas made the buckboard team fast to a bush and at a nod from Hill proceeded to cut pieces from a rawhide lariat and tie the prisoners' hands behind their backs. He herded them over to their fellow captives and tied their legs to the piñon stump.

"About time them Yaquis git down with those hombres from the summit," the cowboy said. His contented look covered the five bound men. "We're sure roundin' 'em, huh, Boss."

"Listen ——" Vince Clayson was still thinking of the feel of Dern's derringer against his spine. "Listen — you mebbe don't know that Jess Kinner and twenty or thirty fellers is combing the chaparral for you, Carnady."

"Gracias." Hill's thoughts were racing, trying to plan his next move. What to do with his prisoners was a problem. Coldwater's jail was not yet a safe place for them. He was not sure that Sam Hally and Seth McGee would arrive in time to combine their forces with Don Julio's Mexicans.

"You won't have a chance if Kinner's bunch picks up your trail," warned the liveryman.

Hill was listening to echoing hoof thuds approaching down the Pass. Justo and Atilano, coming with their prisoners. He came to a decision. The secret hideout cave was the only answer — the one safe place where he could hold these men. He was in a fever to be on his way back to the ranch, to his grandfather — to Ellen Dunbar.

Justo and Atilano appeared round the bend, each with a horse on a lead-rope. Ace Roan was riding double with one of the prisoners. The three men were securely roped to their saddles and looked very dejected.

Hill shook his head as Kansas and Bill Wallace started to dismount them. "We're riding them over to the cave," he said. "Kansas, you get the other men mounted on their horses."

"Curly will have to ride double with one of 'em," Kansas said. "Vince Clayson, too, I reckon — and that leaves Dern."

"The blacks is saddle-broke," Vince informed them. He was desperately eager to cultivate their favour. "Dern and I can ride 'em bareback."

"A man lies dead in the Pass," Justo said in Spanish to Hill.

"He is very dead," Atilano said.

"Strawly," muttered Ace Roan. He looked inquiringly at Vince and Dern.

"Dern shot him," Vince told him. "I'm finished with Dern. He's a killin' wolf."

"He sure got us in a mess," grumbled Ace. "I went up there round that first bend and run into one of these Yaquis . . . had his gun on me before I even spotted him. The other fellers was already tied up at the spring where we left 'em watering their broncs."

The blacks were unhitched from the buckboard, harness stripped and the buckboard pushed from sight behind the bushes. Bill Wallace and Kansas boosted Dern up on one of the horses. Vince needed no help. Their legs were retied and the horses put on lead-ropes.

Dern spoke his first words. "You can't get away with this, Carnady. I've got men coming on the jump from Coyote Wells, and Kinner is already smelling out your trail. Coldwater will be too hot for you and Don Julio. You haven't a chance."

"Boss!" Kansas reached for his gun. "Let me fix the skunk right now."

Hill shook his head. "Let's ride." He turned to his own horse. He wanted above all things to be on his way to the ranch. "You know the short-cuts back to the cave, Kansas?"

"You ain't coming with us?" Kansas showed worry. "Eight fellers is quite a bunch for me and Bill to handle."

"Justo and Atilano will go along with you." Hill looked at the Yaqui twins. "Or must you return at once to Don Julio's *casa*?" he asked in Spanish.

They shook their heads. "*El Señor* promise he will have our ears if we return without the Americano señorita," Justo told him. "We go where you go — to find the señorita."

"*Por esta cruz!*" Atilano crossed thumb and forefinger. "It is so!"

"I'm going to the ranch." Hill stepped into his saddle. "Pick up my trail there, but first help get these men to the cave where Pablo keeps watch on the other one."

Bill Wallace said uneasily. "You're taking a big risk, Carnady — going to the ranch — alone — and this Kinner bunch on the prowl for you." The adamant resolve on Hill's face told him that further argument was useless. His hand lifted in a parting gesture. "Come on, Kansas — let's get these men over to that hiding place of yours."

Hill waited until they disappeared round a bend of the shallow ravine, the two Yaquis trailing them, rifles across saddles, eyes alert. He would like to have gone with them. The cave was actually quite close to the ranch house, but getting there from the Loop meant a detour of two or three miles. He could save valuable time by following the willow brakes to the horse pasture.

He glanced up at the sun. Hardly more than two hours since he had surprised Kickapoo at his post under the bedroom window. The chances were even the man's disappearance would not be discovered for several hours, not until it was time for him to be relieved. Kickapoo had admitted that Kinner had left only three or four men to keep watch at the ranch house. The important thing was to get there before Kinner returned from his futile search. It was even possible that Kinner might first go to Coldwater for a conference with Dern, only to learn that Dern had either fled or was on his way to the ranch. A desirable possibility that would give him more time, and it was time he needed — and the element of surprise. He would have to meet things as they came, use his wits — and hope for the best.

Hill thought of Ellen Dunbar as he swung the bay horse into the concealing willow brakes of the Rio San Jacinto. He knew, now, that she had become very precious to him.

Chapter Sixteen

Footsteps in the hall, the rasp of key in lock, drew Ellen upright on the bed. The door opened, revealed Bat Savan's morose face. It was plain he was in an ugly mood. He stood aside to let Teresa enter the room. The woman gave the girl a warm smile and went to the table.

"Bueno!" she exclaimed, looking at the empty plate. "You 'ave eat nize, Señorita."

Ellen got to her feet. "You are a good cook, Teresa. Thank you for everything."

"Get a move on you," growled Bat. "That Doc Larny feller has taken close on five *pesos* from me and I'm wantin' back in the game before he's so drunk he'll pass out on me."

Ellen guessed from his bloodshot eyes, his heavy tongue, that Bat had been doing some drinking himself. She decided it was best not to detain Teresa, further arouse his ill humour.

The Mexican woman must have been of the same opinion. She silently gathered up the dishes and turned to the door.

"W'en it comes noon I breeng more," she said as she passed the girl. "*Adios,* Señorita. You 'ave nize sleep."

The door closed with a slam behind them, the key scraped in lock and their footsteps faded down the hall.

Ellen went to the window, her thoughts again on that shadow she had glimpsed in the bushes beyond the sentry under her window. She had been so sure that something had stirred there.

Surprise widened her eyes as she gazed down at the big tree. Kickapoo had disappeared. Her eyes lifted, probed deeper into the grove, and suddenly she saw him, stumbling away, a man close at his back, prodding him with a gun. Her heart almost stopped, began to race. The man with a gun looked like a Mexican vaquero, only she knew he was not a Mexican. That tall, easy-striding body — the sunlit glint of red in his hair — the brief glimpse of a face she had come to love. She had not been mistaken those few minutes earlier. It was Hill Carnady's shadow she had seen in the bushes.

The two men vanished. She wondered what Hill was planning to do. It seemed impossible for him to do anything. She tried to reassure herself. Nothing was impossible for Hill Carnady. She had already seen him in action.

It was very still in the big ranch yard. No life stirred there, no sound of voices from the bunkhouse. It might be hours before Jess Kinner and his men returned from their manhunt. The thought of the cold-eyed foreman sent a shiver through her. He was searching for Hill — *combing the chaparral,* and his gun, and the guns of his riders each carried a death warrant for the man she loved. Hill was deliberately risking his life for his grandfather — and for her. She liked to think that she was in his thoughts, too. He would know by now that Oswen Dern had sent her to the ranch house. It was even possible he had glimpsed her face in the window. He would be back — and she must be ready — ready to help with every ounce of wit and courage in her.

She wished Teresa could know that Hill was so close. Teresa would know ways to help, too. She could carry a little secret message of cheer and hope to old Captain Carnady.

Ellen shook her head. Too many useless conjectures tumbling through her mind. She must keep her mind cool and fast-thinking, not surrender to hysterical excitement.

She drew a chair to the window and sat down, tried hard to keep impatience from darkening her hopes. The minutes passed — an hour. She could hardly bear it. An hour gone and no sign of Hill. Despite her resolve, fear seized her again. Kinner's riders had picked up Hill's trail. She could think of no other reason why he should not have returned. Hill was dead — *dead.*

She sprang from the chair, began to pace the floor, and suddenly her distressed eyes saw something on the table where Teresa had piled the dishes before taking them away. A string of simple wooden beads with a little silver cross — *a rosary.*

Ellen gazed at it. Teresa was bidding her to pray. It was the only help she could give her. Teresa was praying, too. Which explained why she had been able to live through the horrors of the past weeks — keep that look of quiet courage, and peace — and hope, in her kindly face.

Tears filled the girl's eyes. She shook them away, picked up the string of beads, touched them uncertainly. She had never used a rosary, and she stood for a long moment, trying to recall some words a friend of her school days had used. *Hail, Mary! Full of Grace, the Lord is with thee. . . .*

She gave up, repeated the Lord's Prayer, holding the little silver cross to her heart. She said another little prayer for Hill Carnady, somewhere out in the chaparral, fighting for the life of his grandfather — for her life, too.

Courage flowed back to her. She sat down again in the chair by the window — let time go by without too much thinking. No sound of life yet stirred from the ranch yard. Kinner and his riders had not returned. She could tell by the sun that noon was not far away. Two hours and more had passed since that brief and wonderful glimpse of Hill. Her fingers caressed the string of beads; and suddenly he was under the window, looking up at her, warning finger on his lips.

Ellen could hardly believe her eyes. His approach had been so soundless she had not dreamed he was so near. She got carefully out of the chair, heedful of the warning he had sent her. It seemed to her that a miracle had happened. Her fingers touched the string of little wooden beads — Teresa's blessed rosary. They were so warm, full of the fire of new-born hope.

Standing back from the window, her cautious sidelong look on the man below, she saw him climbing up the sheer wall. It was beyond belief. She could see nothing for his hands to grasp, and yet he was almost instantly crawling through the open window. He sank into the chair, his breath coming in short gasps. She could only gaze at him, wide-eyed, her own breath keeping time to her fast-beating heart.

He gave her the warm smile she remembered from the night when her Thanksgiving hymn had brought him to her homestead door. He had not been sure of the light in the window. A house where no house had been when he had left the ranch for his studies at the Colorado School of Mines. She had not known he was Captain Carnady's grandson until after he rescued her from the men who had put the torch to the homestead.

He was on his feet, looking at her. "Ellen — something happened — when you opened the door to me night before last."

"Yes," she said. "Something happened to both of us." And she added, wonder in her voice. "Only night before last, Hill? It seems years!"

"Yes — it seems years and years ——" His arms were holding her close. "Ellen — *Ellen* ——"

She pushed him away. "Hill — our first kiss — our first glimpse of heaven!"

He was looking at the string of beads, still

291

in her fingers. "Teresa's rosary!"

"Yes," Ellen said. "I'm keeping it forever and ever. It saved my sanity."

"I gave Teresa that rosary years ago, a birthday present." A reminiscent smile softened the grim set of his face. "I was only a kid, then."

"I'm keeping it forever and ever," Ellen repeated. "Where I go, this rosary will go with me." She held the silver cross to her lips. "Teresa's rosary saved me from going mad, Hill." Her hand held him back. "No — Hill! Listen — Teresa is coming soon with my noon meal — and Bat Savan will be with her." She saw by his expression that he was remembering Bat Savan.

"We'll have a surprise for him." He went quickly to the closet, opened the door and disappeared inside, reappeared with a short rawhide lariat. "My first rope when I was a kid," he told her with another reminiscent smile. "I never expected to use it again." He examined it briefly, tossed it back into the closet and closed the door.

"Hill ——" She went to the window, peered down at the sheer wall. "How in the world did you climb up?"

"Secret hand-holes I made when I was a kid. I've climbed up and down that wall a lot of times." He was at her side, looking off towards the ranch yard. Ellen read his thoughts.

"I heard Kickapoo talking to the man he relieved," she told him. "He said that Jess Kinner was leaving with his men for another attempt to find you."

Hill nodded. "I know, but he may be back soon — unless he goes into Coldwater."

"Kickapoo was one of the men who burned the house," Ellen said. "I saw you taking him away, your gun in his back." Her voice choked. "Oh, Hill — you were so long coming back. I began to imagine all sorts of dreadful things." She held up the rosary. "It was this that gave me strength — gave me hope."

"Kickapoo is where he's safe for the Law ——" Hill hesitated. "A lot has happened since you ran away from the *casa* ——"

"I didn't *really* run away," defended Ellen. "I slipped away just to have a talk with Oswen Dern." She faltered. "I — I didn't dream that he was — was such a monster."

He was looking curiously at her gay skirt, the low-cut white silk bodice, the red slippers. "Delfina's?" he asked.

Ellen nodded, her expression contrite. "She was so nice to me . . . I'm ashamed to think of the worry I caused her — and all of them."

293

"A girl staying at the hotel, Lucy Royale, rode into the desert that same morning," Hill went on. "She was wearing levis, blue flannel shirt — a white Stetson ——"

"I'll bet she got it from Jake Kurtz," interrupted Ellen. "That's where I got mine."

"It seems that she did." Hill's tone was grim. "The trouble is, Whitey was hanging around, looking for you. He saw this girl riding away and followed her, thinking she was you. In the meantime, Don Julio's Yaquis were looking for you. They arrived in time to save Miss Royale. They took her back to the *casa,* thinking she was you because of the clothes, so like the outfit you were wearing when we arrived there at sun-up. Delfina, of course, guessed the truth immediately. The Yaquis, Miss Royale's fiancé, Bill Wallace, and another man, were sent off to pick up my trail and tell me that you were probably a prisoner here."

"I'm so ashamed," Ellen repeated. "I certainly acted like a little fool." She was silent for a moment, then — "What happened to Whitey?"

"Justo and Atilano left him out there in the brush — for the buzzards."

Ellen was very pale. She was thinking of what might have happened to the other girl. "He was terrible," she said.

"You can forget him ——" Hill drew her close. "And Ellen — here is more important news — "I've got Oswen Dern, and some of his friends where Kickapoo is — all safe for the Law to deal with."

Astonishment held her wordless. He told her about the meeting with Bill Wallace and the others, their news that Dern was heading for the ranch.

"We trapped them in Hell Pass. It's the end for Dern. He's finished in the San Jacinto."

"Oh, Hill!" She clung to him.

"Sam Hally and Seth McGee and the others are on their way to Coldwater. Dick will be with them. You don't need to worry about him any more."

"I still don't understand why Dern sent those men to burn the homestead," she wondered.

"He thought there was gold there." Hill was studying a faint haze of dust a mile or two beyond the horse pasture. A second dust haze drew his attention, more distant and beyond the river. Kinner and his riders. Another half hour would see them back at the ranch. He heard Ellen's questioning voice.

"Gold — *gold* at Red Butte Springs?"

"Not gold," Hill told her. "His mining

expert, Lucy Royale's father, says Red Butte is loaded with copper — a bonanza."

"It won't do me any good now," Ellen said. "I'm sure that Oswen Dern never filed my homestead papers." Her eyes were very bright as she looked at him. "I don't care for myself, Hill. I'm thinking about Dick."

"It will work out," he reassured her. "Dern won't live long enough to claim Red Butte Springs, or any part of the ranch."

She was reminded of Captain Carnady. "Your grandfather," she said. "Teresa says he's had a stroke — lies in bed."

"I know. Kickapoo told me ——" He was listening intently. "Somebody coming ——"

"Teresa," she whispered. "Bat Savan will be with her."

Hill drew his gun and moved close to the wall where the opening door would conceal him. Ellen, her heart beating fast, looked around helplessly, not knowing what to do. He motioned to the chair. She sat down, angry at herself for the weakness in her legs.

The footsteps drew close, the key turned in the lock and the door flew open. Teresa came in, a tray in her hands. *"Buenas tardes, Señorita."* She crossed over to the table, a hint of alarm in her eyes as she sensed the girl's nervousness. "I breeng nize food," she said.

Bat Savan remained framed in the doorway, hand on the gun in his holster. He was quite drunk. Ellen got out of the chair. She must do something to draw the man further into the room, give Hill a chance to step from behind the door. She gestured at the wash basin.

"More water," she managed to say.

"Huh?" The man lurched into the room. "I sure am tired of fetchin' water for you."

There was too much at stake to waste time. Hill slid from behind the door, swung the steel barrel of the .45 against Bat's head. He caught the man as he fell, lowered his limp body to the floor. Ellen ran to the closet, pulled the door open and snatched at the rawhide lariat. She threw it at Hill, then hurried to the hall door, removed the key and locked the door from the inside. The weakness had left her knees. She stood there, watched with hard, bright eyes while Hill quickly bound the unconscious man. He finished the job by contriving an efficient gag with Bat's own soiled bandana.

His look went to the girl. "Thanks, Ellen, for thinking of the door." He bent over the bound man, stripped off his holster and gun, dragged him inside the closet, closed and locked the door, pocketing the key.

Teresa came out of her trance. *"Madre de*

Dios! Hillito — muchacho mio."

He gave her a quick hug. "How is he, Teresa?"

She understood the question. "*El Señor* mooch gooder." She broke into a torrent of Spanish. "The good God has sent you in time. Your grandfather is well again, but fears to let them know. He has always said you would come."

His gesture silenced her. "How many more of them downstairs?" he asked in Spanish.

"Two, and the doctor, who is very drunk and helpless. One man guards your grandfather." She thought a moment. "Perhaps two or three asleep in the bunkhouse — and soon there will be Señor Kinner and his vaqueros."

Hill went to the window again. The larger dust haze was approaching fast. The second dust haze had vanished. It might have been made by Justo and Atilano. Once close to the ranch house they would be careful not to let dust betray them. They were Yaquis, wary and cunning and alert. He rather hoped his guess was correct. He could use Justo and Atilano. He was conscious, too, of a longing for Sam Hally and Seth McGee and all the old-timers they might have been able to round up. Perhaps it had been a mistake to send word by Juanito for them to go to Coldwater. He was needing those fighting old longhorns. Coldwater could have waited a few hours.

He took another look at the approaching dust haze. Another twenty-five minutes would see Kinner's men in the ranch yard. He must do some fast thinking.

Teresa was babbling Spanish at him. "I did not know you when you burst from behind the door. I thought you were a vaquero."

His gesture again silenced her. "Can my grandfather walk?"

"Si ——"

"We will go down to his room together," Hill continued in Spanish. "If I am seen you will say that I am a new vaquero Señor Dern has sent to keep watch under the girl's window."

"Si ——" Excitement burned in Teresa's dark eyes.

"I'll take care of that man, once we get inside the room." Hill slid Bat's gun from its holster, held it out to Ellen. "Lock the door when we leave, and don't open for any voice but mine or Teresa's."

"Yes," Ellen said. "I understand." She took the long-barrelled .45, followed them to the

door. Hill turned the key, held the door
open and followed Teresa into the hall.

Chapter Seventeen

Ellen closed the door and turned the key. She felt a bit light-headed again. Things moved too fast. She had never known a man like Hill Carnady — his lightning mind — his instant decisions. She looked down at her hands. One held a heavy .45 colt — the other a rosary. She went slowly to the bed, sat down where she could watch both doors. Bat Savan lay behind the closet door, securely tied and gagged, but she was taking no chances with him. He was the leader of the trio who had so ruthlessly put the torch to the new home she and Dick had made for themselves. Whitey was dead, Kickapoo was Hill's prisoner, and now Bat Savan, for the moment, was *her* prisoner.

All seemed very still in the house, but now she heard the thud of approaching hoofs. Jess Kinner and his riders. Terror mounted in her. She looked again at what she held in her hands — a gun — and rosary.

Those hoof-beats were coming closer so fast, too dreadfully fast, and not a sound from below stairs. Hill and Teresa were down there. She hardly dared to think of what was happening.

Ellen's gaze clung to the little string of wooden beads with its silver cross. She laid the heavy six-gun in her lap, lifted Teresa's rosary to her breast. *"Hail, Mary!"* she whispered, *"Full of Grace, the Lord is with thee . . ."*

While she sat there, the rosary clasped to her heart, she heard the rush and trample of shod hoofs in the ranch yard, the bantering shouts of the men as they off-saddled, the harsh voice of Jess Kinner.

"Shorty — you wrangle a fresh string from the horse pasture."

"Have a heart, Jess!" protested a weary rider. "I'm sure fed up plenty with scoutin' round for that Carnady feller."

"We're heading for Dark Canyon just as quick as you boys has et," the HC foreman told them. "And don't give me any of your lip."

"Like looking for a needle in a haystack," grumbled another voice.

"Dark Canyon is the only place we haven't tried," Kinner said. "I'll tell the cook you boys will be right in as soon as you've washed up."

Ellen snatched the gun from her lap and hurried to the window. She could see the men turning their horses into the corral, and Kinner, walking across the big yard towards the ranch house. Her heart stood still. No word yet from Hill, still downstairs. Kinner would be almost sure to have a look at Captain Carnady and almost just as certain to see how the girl prisoner was faring. It seemed that Hill was faced with immediate disaster. The tall foreman passed from her view, but she could hear the crunch of his boot heels, the rasp of spurs.

Her gaze lifted, followed the man, Shorty, riding into the horse pasture. His companions were trooping towards the bunkhouse under the big cottonwood trees. One of them had already seized a wash basin and was filling it from the hand pump at the water trough. They, too, would soon be hurrying to the house, to the long dining-room used by HC's cowboys. She counted them. More than half a score. How could Hill cope with them, single-handed!

Something drew her attention. A faint haze of dust beyond the great grove of trees opposite her window. There was no wind blowing to lift dust. Her eyes widened. Only horses would be making that dust. More men were approaching the ranch-house, perhaps the rest of Kinner's outfit. She recalled that he had ridden away that early dawn with more than twice the number of men now gathering at the bunkhouse.

Ellen stood there, watching, wondering. Yes, those nearing riders could only be more of Kinner's men. Not help coming — *not an answer to her prayers.*

The jingle of Kinner's spurs reached her from the kitchen porch steps, and she was about to turn away from the window, of a mind to disobey Hill's injunctions not to leave the room. He was needing help, and she had a gun in her hand. A movement in the bushes beyond the big tree held her motionless, a flitting shape — two shapes, and even at that distance she recognized those tall steeple hats. She had last seen them on the heads of the two Yaquis she had tricked when she had slipped away from the safety of Don Julio's high walls. *Justo and Atilano.* She was not mistaken. Those two fierce fighting men were close — had come to help.

She started to run to the door, came to a standstill. Hill had told her not to leave the room. She had disobeyed him once, to her sorrow. Dare she again ignore his injunctions, make things even more difficult for him? He wanted her safe from possible

304

harm. And he was not alone now. Not with Justo and Atilano so near.

Ellen slowly went back to the window to keep watch. She slipped the string of wooden beads around her neck, held the silver cross to her heart. . . . That approaching dust was certainly made by horsemen — a lot of them. . . .

Jess Kinner was in an ugly mood. More than half of his men had decided to say *adios* to the ranch and make dust back to their border haunts. All of them were wanted by the Law for various crimes and they were not liking the fact that Hill Carnady was on the loose. The Carnadys were known as dangerous men to tangle with, and Sam Hally and Seth McGee. The failure to locate them had aroused justifiable fears for their own necks. He was inclined to follow their example, head for the Panhandle with the few men who still remained loyal to him. But first there were certain affairs to be settled with Oswen Dern. He distrusted Dern, suspected the lawyer's intentions regarding himself. There had been a verbal agreement to give him a half ownership in the ranch, once old Carnady had signed the desired papers. Kinner doubted that Dern intended to keep the promise. There was one way he could profit from the situation. Dern had left the management of the ranch in his hands and he had taken care to gradually push all the best cattle across the river to HC's West Side range, some two thousand head of two and three year olds. He could, within a couple of days, push them over the border and get a fair price for them, pay off his few remaining riders and make tracks for Mexico City. If his last attempt to find Hill Carnady in the Dark Canyon country failed, he too would say *adios* to Dern and the ranch — make for the border with his plunder.

He slammed through the kitchen door, gave the stout Mexican woman at the stove a sour look. "Get some grub on the table for the boys, Rosa. We're in a rush."

"Si, Señor," the cook said. "I 'ave beeg stew all ready — the coffee made — and fresh pie."

Kinner looked at her thoughtfully. "Put up a couple of dozen beef sandwiches. We may have to stay out all night." He was thinking, *I must tell the boys to get their blanket rolls and tarps.*

"Si, Señor ——" She poured him a cup of coffee from the steaming pot.

"Gracias." Kinner gulped the hot brew, wiped his mouth with shirt sleeve. "Where's Teresa — and the others?"

"They weeth old señor in hees room," Rosa informed him. "Old señor moch seek ____"

Kinner nodded, put down the cup and turned to the door. The Mexican woman's look followed him. She spat at his vanishing back. "Peeg," she muttered under her breath.

He strode down the hall, his mind busy, going over his plans. Captain Carnady was a problem he would leave to Oswen Dern. If the old man died, so much the better. As for the girl — Kinner shook his head. To much at stake to waste time with excess baggage, no matter how attractive. Once he was on the run he would have to keep moving fast.

Without troubling to knock he pushed into the room that for years had been old Captain Carnady's bedroom. Too late his hands reached for the gun in his holster.

"Keep 'em up high, Kinner."

The foreman gazed with aghast eyes at the man who looked like a Mexican vaquero with red in his hair and whose gun menaced him with instant death.

Another man sat on the edge of the big bed, a big, gaunt man with shaggy hair and blazing deep-set eyes. He too held a gun in a hand as steady as a rock. And back in a corner was Teresa, a triumphant smile on her face, a gun in her hand.

The old man on the bed spoke. "A little surprise party for you, Kinner," he rumbled. "Hill — take his guns. I've got him covered, and I'm craving to pull trigger."

Hill deftly removed the ashen-faced man's guns. "I'd like to kill you, Kinner," he said in a tight voice. "I'm leaving it to the Law to hang you, alongside Dern and the rest of your friends."

"Tie him up, Hill," rumbled Cap Carnady from his bedside. "Take no chances. Hog-tie him like those other scoundrels."

Kinner's dazed look wavered at the two bound and gagged men lying on the floor, against the far wall. On a small cot under a window he saw Doc Larney, helplessly drunk, but also securely tied.

"They weren't expecting me to walk in on them, Kinner. Nothing they could do about it." Hill gestured for the foreman to stretch out on the floor, face down. Hill tied his hands behind his back, drew a tight noose over his ankles and turned him over so he lay face up.

"You ain't getting away with this," Kinner mouthed. "I've got a dozen men out there. They'll blast you out of this room."

Hill held the gun within an inch of his

face. "One yell, mister, and you'll be very dead."

"I'm not yellin'," Kinner mumbled. "I'm only telling you what you're up against."

"I'll say you're not yelling!" Hill snatched the man's bandana, tied it firmly over his mouth, stuffing it hard between his lips.

"Heave him alongside the others," suggested Cap Carnady. "Give me those guns you took off him."

Hill dragged Kinner over to the wall, handed the long-barrelled 45's to his grandfather.

"Now, boy," chuckled the old cowman. "You go think up something to do with the rest of those damn border thugs. I can watch over this mangy bunch." He waggled two heavy guns.

Hill was staring with startled eyes at a side window facing on the grove of trees. A face was pressed there, a face under a tall steeple hat. *Justo.* He said, softly, "I think we have help, Grandfather." He looked at Teresa. "See if you can get upstairs . . . tell Miss Dunbar how things are going."

Teresa nodded that she understood, took a look into the hall and slipped through the door. Hill threw the bolt, looked at the window again. Another face there — *Atilano.* The two Yaquis had kept their promise to follow his trail to the ranch.

He went to the bound Kinner, gazed down at him. "Listen, we picked up Dern and some of his friends in Hell Pass. You'll get no help from him, Kinner. He's finished — and so are you." He went quickly to the window, slid it open and peered outside. The two Yaquis were waiting, vague shapes in the bushes.

"What do you see, boy?" asked his grand-father.

"Friends ——" Hill looked back at him. "If you must shoot, shoot to kill."

"I have three guns here," the old cowman told him with a grim smile. "And I don't miss my shots, boy."

Hill said, briefly. "I'll be back ——" He dropped soundlessly from sight. . . .

Ellen recognized Teresa's soft voice outside the door. She turned the key and the Mexican woman slipped inside the room, locked the door behind her. *"Señorita!"* Her voice was jubilant. "Our *Hillito* say breeng you beeg news. Those *malo* hombre all tie up and old *señor* now ees save from them ——"

Ellen was dragging her to the window. "Teresa — *Teresa* —— *look* ——"

The Mexican woman babbled on. "*Hillito* 'ave that *malo* Kinner all tie up ——" She

310

broke into excited Spanish that Ellen was unable to understand.

"Look!" repeated the girl. "Teresa — those men — they are friends! My *brother, Dick,* rides with them ——"

"Ave Maria Purisima!" exclaimed Hill's old nurse. She crossed herself. *"Señor* Hally and *Señor* McGee, and our good vaqueros, ride in answer to our prayers, *Señorita mia!"*

Gunfire rattled from downstairs, shouts, curses — agonized yells. Ellen tore her gaze from the fast approaching horsemen and ran to the door. Before Teresa could prevent, she had turned the key and was in the hall. Gun clutched in hand, the old Mexican woman hurried after the girl in time to see Hill intercept her at the foot of the stairs.

"It's all over, Ellen!" Hill holstered his gun, took the girl in his arms. "Justo and Atilano have the men trapped in the dining-room. There was some shooting — but they've dropped their guns — given up."

"But, Hill ——" Excitement, his embrace, left her breathless. "Dick is coming — a lot of them — old Don Julio and Delfina ——"

They rushed through the kitchen where Atilano stood at the men's dining-room door, his rifle menacing the remnants of Jess Kinner's outfit. They dashed past the big tankhouse and came to a standstill under the cottonwoods.

Dick Dunbar was the first down from his horse, and for a moment Ellen had no eyes for anybody else. She clung to her tall young brother. "They told me you were dying, perhaps dead," she told him tearfully. "Oh, Dick!"

Sam Hally and Seth McGee were pushing through the crowding dusty-faced cowboys. The Bar 2 partners wore wide grins.

"Well, son," rumbled Sam. "We wasn't needin' to head for Coldwater like you said. We nabbed Steff Hancy on his way to Coyote Wells to round up a bunch of fellers to help him run Don Julio out of town. We got Steff back in that cave of yours along with Dern and the other fellers."

"Kansas stayed back with Juanito and Pablo and a couple of the boys to keep watch on 'em," chuckled Seth McGee. His cherubic face was suddenly a grim, hard mask. "Mat Webster is bringing the U.S. Marshal from Hatchita to take care of Dern's bunch of killers. They should be in before sundown."

"We've got a few more in the house, including Jess Kinner," Hill informed them.

"We'll take care of them now," Sam said. He hesitated, keen eyes probing the younger man. "How is Cap makin' out, son?"

Hill chuckled. "Right now he's sitting on his bed, holding a couple of .45's on Kinner and a pair of other coyotes we nabbed."

Sam grinned. "Come on, fellers!" he called to the group of attentive cowboys. "Let's get our ropes on these mavericks Hill's got rounded up in the house."

Boot heels crunched, spurs rasped, as the grinning men followed him round the tank-house to the kitchen porch. Hill became aware of Ellen's voice.

"Hill —— my brother, Dick ——"

"I've been hearing a lot about you," young Dunbar said as they clasped hands.

Hill was smiling into the girl's eyes. "Ellen will be telling you something more about me, Dick. Something about both of us."

Dust trailed another group of riders coming fast up the avenue. In the lead was Don Julio Severa, erect in a resplendent silver-mounted saddle on a golden horse with flowing silver mane and tail. Delfina accompanied him, riding side-saddle and waving excitedly as she caught sight of Ellen. Behind them, three abreast, rode Dr. Royale and Bill Wallace with Lucy between them. Lucy still wearing the cowboy garb she had purchased from Jake Kurtz. More than twenty dark-faced vaqueros brought up the rear, rifles in saddle-boots, guns in their belts.

Don Julio halted his horse. "I see that all is well," he said in Spanish to Hill.

"All is well, dear great-uncle," Hill assured him. "It was good of you to come."

Don Julio's benevolent smile told Ellen she had been forgiven. She said, penitently, "Do not be cross with Atilano and Justo. They have been wonderful."

The old hidalgo gestured. "It is well for them they found you, *Señorita.* I would have had their ears."

The Royales and Bill Wallace and Delfina were off their horses and hurrying towards them. Ellen heard her brother's voice, low, admiring. "Who is that little beauty in the riding habit?" She gave him a keen look and what she read in his face made her wonder if Delfina, after all, might also become a rancher's wife. She hoped so. As for the copper bonanza under Red Butte Springs, it could stay there forever for all she cared. It was going to be up to her Hill Carnady to decide what they would do with that copper.

The employees of Thorndike Press hope you have enjoyed this Large Print book. All our Thorndike, Wheeler, and Kennebec Large Print titles are designed for easy reading, and all our books are made to last. Other Thorndike Press Large Print books are available at your library, through selected bookstores, or directly from us.

For information about titles, please call:
  (800) 223-1244

or visit our Web site at:
  http://gale.cengage.com/thorndike

To share your comments, please write:
  Publisher
  Thorndike Press
  10 Water St., Suite 310
  Waterville, ME 04901